GOOD FRIDAY

An armada of Russian aircraft, led by wiley ~~Commander~~ mander Tarpolov, is spotted heading toward the Saudi Arabian oilfields.

GOOD FRIDAY

Marine Commander Tom Hemingway pilots a U.S. aircraft carrier, loaded with combat-ready marines and super-maneuverable Harrier fighters, through the Persian Gulf to oppose them.

GOOD FRIDAY

In Washington, D.C. . . . in Moscow . . . in the Saudi Royal Palace . . . fierce arguments rage and dangerous gambles are taken.

GOOD FRIDAY

The most crucial day the world has ever known blazes toward its high noon of decision. . . .

"AS READABLE AS TOM CLANCY . . . A SMASHINGLY GOOD STORY THAT GRABS YOU AND NEVER LETS GO!"

—*Pacific Flyer Aviation News*

"Gripping . . . fascinating . . . true to life. . . . I loved every minute of GOOD FRIDAY!"

—Dale F. Brown,
author of *Flight of the Old Dog*

GOOD FRIDAY

A NOVEL BY

ROBERT LAWRENCE HOLT

A SIGNET BOOK

NEW AMERICAN LIBRARY

After the pointless slaughter of 1.2 million soldiers (a fifth of whom were 14- to 16-year-old boys of Khomeini's Revolutionary Guards) in a twelve-year war of attrition with Iran, the army of Iraq abandons their strategic port of Basra in disorganized retreat northward.

Two weeks later, the Iranians invade the oil-rich state of Kuwait; and by mid-April, the Iranian army is massed along the Kuwait/Saudi Arabia border . . . their southern advance temporarily halted by an influenza epidemic.

To oppose the 300,000-man Iranian army in Kuwait, the Saudis have moved 45,000 men (three-quarters of their ground forces) to their northern border. The Saudi army is reinforced by the Peninsular Shield—9,000 men in a loosely organized band of military units from neighboring Persian Gulf states.

Riyadh, Saudi Arabia

"Kee-rist! They must be doing at least *a hundred.*"

"Or more," responded the Corporal of the Guard. Both Marines stared at the fast-approaching headlights of the four-vehicle procession. The corporal spoke into the embassy intercom.

"Here come the maniacs!"

The lead vehicle—a jeep 100 yards in front of the others—contained four, white-uniformed men with Uzi machine guns. Its driver braked hard and locked his wheels . . . laying 80 feet of rubber before releasing his foot and twisting the jeep sharply toward the compound gate.

The vehicle, its scorched wheels smoking, slid to a halt barely a foot from the barrier. Its sullen occupants wore the cocked red berets of the Saudi Royal Guard. The jeep's driver gave a perfunctory salute as the man beside him casually swung his Uzi around in the general direction of the Marines. The Corporal of the Guard whipped back an immaculate salute and pressed a button to open the iron gate.

At three-second intervals, the other vehicles roared up in similar fashion . . . each displaying a small green-and-white flag on its bumper. A dark green Buick careened through the gate on two left wheels, followed by a heavily-armored, white Cadillac limousine whose wheels squealed in protest at the high-speed, 90-degree turn.

The driver of the last vehicle, a jeep with a mounted machine gun, misjudged his speed and sideswiped the heavy stone pillar anchoring the iron gate. The man standing at the mounted gun tumbled off the jeep, amid whoops of laughter and jeers from his companions. Rolling on the concrete, the hapless man scrambled to his feet and limped after the procession.

Ambassador Emory Clark met the limousine as it jerked to a stop before the vestibule of the American embassy. A slim, tall New Englander with thinning blonde hair above a high forehead, Clark didn't feel the calm his reserved style suggested. The austere demeanor was carefully cultivated to mask his genuine feelings toward his early morning guest. Years of Middle East duty had taught him to dislike and distrust both the Arabs and Israelis—a general bias making him ideally suited to his post in Riyadh.

An officer of the Royal Guard emerged from the front of the white limousine and opened one of its right rear doors.

Speaking as he pulled his portly, six-foot frame through the door, King Asad sternly inquired, "What is your President going to do?"

Clark was taken aback by the imperative tone, as the roundfaced Saudi king normally displayed a docile and amenable nature. The American recognized both anger and fear on the king's face as the two men stood opposite each other, the eyes of the ambassador on the same level as those of Asad. As one of the shorter sons of Abdul Aziz Al Saud, the founder of the kingdom, Asad always wore elevator shoes in public.

"I don't know, Your Majesty." Clark replied. "President Steiner requested you come here in order to maintain direct communication with the White House." The ambassador checked his watch. It was exactly 45 minutes since the violation of Pakistani airspace had been reported.

They both hurried into the embassy, followed closely by the Royal Guard officer.

After berating their bruised comrade for his fall, the other white-uniformed members of the Royal Guard nervously smoked on the steps of the vestibule . . . making a point to direct the muzzles of their Israeli-made weapons at the two Marines guarding the embassy's entrance.

The two Americans stiffly maintained their brace on either side of the embassy door and traded an air of utter contempt for the ill manners of their guests.

The White House

The muted fluorescent light in the subterranean chamber cast an unhealthy pallor over its denizens . . . who, subdued by the atmosphere, seldom spoke in more than hushed tones. Electronic grid maps covered most of the pale yellow walls of the tennis court-sized, cavernous communications center of the White House. Eight stories directly beneath the Oval Office, it was officially termed the Situation Room for the benefit of the press and public. The twenty-odd men who manned its consoles preferred the more accurate single-syllable and referred to their workplace as the War Room.

"Tell *the professor* to make a decision quick!" crackled over the wall-mounted VCR-110 transceiver. General W. J. Morrison winced as he glanced toward the President and his chief assistant entering the room.

The radio's message abruptly halted the medium-height, paunchy frame of President Allan Steiner. His heavily jowled face, dominated by deceptively soft blue eyes, was topped by a shaggy mane of white hair. Peering over small, rectangular Ben Franklin glasses, he studied Morrison a moment.

"Who the hell was *that?*" the President demanded.

"Admiral Johnston on the Constellation, sir," replied the short, square-faced general. He spoke rapidly in a clipped cadence and wore the intense glare of a small man affirming his authority. A former fighter pilot, Morrison was accustomed to establishing dominance early over others; and he bridled before the President—a person he considered more an adversary than a superior.

"What's going on now?" the President inquired.

"Sir, the flight from Afghanistan left Pakistan airspace 11 minutes ago and turned due west over the Indian Ocean," answered Morrison, pointing to a cluster of flashing red dots on the 14-foot wide grid map of the Middle East. "The Constellation reported the aircraft carry the insignia of the Afghan Air Force."

"Clever bastards," muttered the President.

"They're definitely Russian," continued Morrison. "After turning west, their fighter escort was observed refueling from Soviet tankers tracked out of South Yemen."

"They must be crazy." President Steiner gaped at the imperceptively moving, flashing dots on the wall map. "What the hell are they up to?"

You know damn well what they're up to thought Morrison with a piercing scowl.

Allan Steiner pivoted away from the wall map and shook his head, as if to deny the obvious. Recalling the trial Nikita Khrushchev had given the young Kennedy 30 years earlier, he raised a hand

to knead his forehead and prayed . . . imploring
that this too would prove but a test.

"Sir, I apologize for the fleet commander's choice
of words," offered Morrison hollowly for the admiral's use of the presidential nickname, "but he
does require orders. The Soviet flight is now entering the Gulf of Oman, and they could reach the
coast of Saudi Arabia within two hours." He
paused and boldly added, "I've taken the precaution of ordering the F-18s aboard the Constellation
and Enterprise into the air."

In his dual role as Commander-in-Chief of the
Air Force and a member of the Joint Chiefs of Staff,
W. J. Morrison was the "military duty officer" in
the capital on the eve of this holiday. The President's nominee for secretary of defense had not yet
been confirmed by the Senate, and the undersec-
retary of defense was already on holiday.

In an undertone, the President dryly commented, "Why are you generals always so anxious
to start World War III?"

Morrison locked eyes with President Steiner, refusing to be stared down. He wondered *how in the
world did we elect a history professor to the White House?*

The bantam general raised his voice so it would
be heard easily by others in the War Room. "Mr.
President, are you prepared to hand over Saudi
Arabia to the communists? Our stated mission in
this sector is to safeguard their oil fields."

"You needn't lecture me, General." President
Steiner cloaked his fury with a tight smile. The
briefings before his inauguration had included the
prediction that the Soviet Union would become a
net importer of oil during the current presidential

term. He had received this news with considerable optimism . . . believing the competition for the Free World's excess oil supplies would cause his Russian counterpart to bring a more cooperative attitude to the peace table. Allan Steiner spoke in a disgruntled tone.

"What is the total number of Russian planes involved?"

"The Puzzle Factory"—Morrison reconsidered his choice of words—"Fort Meade reports 40 Ilyushin II-76Ms and 54 MiG-29 Fulcrums left Kandahar in southern Afghanistan shortly after 0200 hours, Saudi Arabia time."

"What are Ilyushins?"

"The Ilyushin II-76M is a troop transport," Morrison explained with a note of disdain, "designed to carry two medium tanks and 140 fully equipped infantrymen."

The presidential assistant, Jim Hoolihan, injected, "That means they could be carrying 5600 men."

"Jim, relay that information to our ambassador in Riyadh," directed the President. "And check to see if the king has joined him." As President Steiner moved closer to the Middle East wall-map, he told Morrison, "Describe the MiG-29 Fulcrum to me."

The general was mildly surprised the President could repeat the full name of the newest Soviet fighter. Allan Steiner had occupied the Oval Office only three months, after serving four terms in the Senate. He had been elected to the White House with a promise to reduce defense spending and pursue serious peace negotiations with Russia. His

knowledge of military matters was limited . . . as
was his popularity among the military.

"Those are fighter aircraft, sir. They're faster
than our F-18s, but not as maneuverable. We believe their weaponry to be comparable to our own."

Morrison received a teletyped message and, after
scanning it, handed the note to the President who
read it aloud.

"Pakistani military transmissions indicate flight
out of Afghanistan intercepted by their F-15s.
They report 12 F-15s lost and claim one Fulcrum
destroyed."

"That's good news, Mr. President!" exclaimed
the elated general. "If Pakistan's F-15s can shoot
them down, we *certainly* can."

The President frowned. "General, this is *not* good
news. If the Soviets are willing to fight their way
through Pakistani airspace, they are likely to do the
same over Saudi Arabia."

The blank expression of incomprehension on
Morrison's face only served to further annoy the
President, who addressed his assistant.

"Jim, where is General Steel? I want the JCS
Chairman down here immediately!"

"He's on his way," Hoolihan replied. "He
should arrive any minute."

"And where's Clayton Walters?" the President
demanded.

"I'll check on his arrival," Hoolihan responded.
He hurried to the telephones on the circular conference table that dominated the center of the War

Room as the President returned his attention to Morrison.

"What do we have in the Persian Gulf to oppose the Soviets, General?"

"Our Middle East Force—one helicopter assault carrier, three destroyers, and two frigates—lying 35 miles off the coast of Saudi Arabia directly east of Dhahran." For the President's benefit, he added, "Dhahran Air Base controls the Saudi oil fields."

"That's not much of a force," grimaced President Steiner. "It sounds more like a *patrol.*"

Morrison spoke with emphasis. "The assault carrier is the Puller, sir. She carries a complement of 1800 Marines, 24 Sea Stallion helicopters, plus 9 Harrier fighter/attack aircraft."

After a thoughtful pause, the President unwillingly asked, "How effective would our Harriers be against the Fulcrums?"

Having considered the question already, Morrison lamely offered: "I'm not sure, sir."

"Well . . . *goddamn it,*" the President exploded. He deliberately raised his voice to even the score. "If *you* can't answer my questions"—he looked expansively about the room—"who in the hell around here can?"

"The Harriers on the Puller," Morrison testily replied, "are primarily ground-support aircraft and are not designed to optimally engage fighters such as the Fulcrums." He lowered his voice. "If we give the Puller orders soon enough, they could be outfitted with Sidewinders."

"What would that accomplish, General?"

This time Morrison weighed his answer carefully. "We might be able to delay the Soviet flight but not stop it."

"How long a delay?"

Morrison knew the Sidewinders of the Harriers would be no match for the longer-range missiles certainly carried by the Fulcrums . . . if the Soviets played it conservative. With little conviction, he answered, "Maybe ten . . . fifteen minutes."

"What *good* is ten or fifteen minutes?"

Morrison opened his mouth to reply, but was cut off by the President. "Why isn't the Constellation or Enterprise in the Persian Gulf?"

"You can't operate conventional aircraft carriers in a body of water that small" Morris replied condescendingly. "Their flight operations require more room. Plus, the entire eastern shoreline of the Gulf is Iranian." *Dammit*, thought Morrison, *we're wasting precious time while I teach military basics to a president.*

"Then why's the Puller in the Persian Gulf?" queried the President.

"The Harriers on the Puller are V/STOLs, sir. They can take off and land vertically, permitting the Puller to remain stationary on the western side of the Gulf."

"Didn't we sell the Saudis some modern fighters five or six years ago?"

"Yes, sir. They've bought F-15s from us . . . and Tornados from our Nato allies, but Congress wouldn't approve the sale of long-range missiles to go with them so they'd probably be outgunned."

Recalling his repeated votes against the selling of Sparrow missiles to the Arabs, the President tugged at his ear. "I suppose we'd better tell the Puller to prepare for the Soviets."

"Sir, what will be their rules of engagement?"

President Steiner studied Morrison skeptically.

"Who fires first?" explained the general. "The commander of the Harriers should be told this before his planes are launched." Morrison paused. "Or does it matter?"

Of course it matters thought the President. Dropping his head pensively, he walked back to the conference table and sat down. Allan Steiner was a president often described as "a man of circumstance." He hadn't sought the Oval Office with the fervor of his predecessors; in fact, intimates knew he had been downright reluctant to accept the candidacy of his party, preferring to remain in the relative comfort of his Senate seat. When he'd protested his lack of training for the job, it had quickly been pointed out how little preparation most of the contemporary occupants of the White House had received, and he had to agree with his boosters when they told him a background as a professor of history was far better than that of a PT-boat commander, a poker player, a peanut farmer, or an actor.

His election campaign had stressed a "breath of fresh air" for the nation, a welcome change from the politician image of other candidates. His boosters also sensed the voters were ready for a change for the sake of change—that intuitive trait voters in democracies exhibit whenever they feel their country has simply had enough of one bent.

The President looked up at General Morrison and wearily said, "I need time to think this through."

"With due respect, sir . . . there *is* no more time."

President Steiner stared straight ahead, acting as if he hadn't heard the remonstrance.

"The Joint Chiefs have discussed possible options," Morrison calmly continued, "in the event of these confrontations, sir. We've concluded the best solutions are *limited reactions.*"

"What do you mean?" the President responded after a pause.

"Rather than engage the entire Soviet flight, we call their bluff by downing only a single aircraft. While doing this, we make it obvious to them that our action is limited . . . that we do not wish an expanded conflict."

President Steiner leaned back and crossed his arms. "Have we or anyone else *ever tried* such a stratagem with the Soviets?"

Not wishing to reply in the negative, Morrison said, "We haven't had the opportunity yet."

"What if the Soviets aren't bluffing, General?"

Morrison looked aside momentarily.

"I may have been elected on a peace platform, General, but I'm no stranger to the Soviets. They've *overreacted* to provocations throughout their history, particularly during this century." The President's tone turned incredulous. *"Now,* you want me to believe they won't overreact this time also?"

The Chairman of the Joint Chiefs of Staff strode into the War Room. In his three-piece civilian suit, General J. Robert Steel looked more the statesman than a military professional for 41 years. A dark-bristled mustache gave his patrician face a youthful appearance. The only replacement on the JCS since the new administration had taken office, he had been selected due to his open support of the President's peace initiatives.

General Steel went directly to the Middle East grid map after greeting the President. Morrison and President Steiner followed, the latter explaining, "Bob, there are about 5600 Soviet troops less than two hours from the border of Saudi Arabia. Their transports are protected by 53 MiGs. General Morrison tells me neither the Saudi Air Force nor our Harriers in the Gulf can stop them."

Steel directed his first question to Morrison. "Have the F-18s on the Enterprise and Constellation been launched?"

"Yes, sir. They're approximately twenty-eight minutes behind the Soviet flight."

"Raise them on the board," Steel ordered. A short moment after Morrison spoke to a console technician, a cluster of flashing blue dots appeared approximately one foot behind the red dots. When Morrison returned to his side, the JCS Chairman asked him, "Can they overtake the Soviet flight before it arrives over Saudi Arabia?"

"They could," offered Morrison, "but the fuel expended would severely limit their engagement time." The Air Force general correctly assumed Admiral Johnston in the Indian Ocean had ordered his fighters in immediate pursuit after launching, skipping the routine aerial refueling following their catapult shots.

"Order the F-18s to catch up," commanded Steel. "We need their option."

Gratified the JCS Chairman hadn't bothered to

consult the President on the matter, Morrison swiftly wrote out a message on his clipboard. After handing it to a communications officer, Morrison reminded Steel, "Sir, both the F-18s and Harriers need their rules of engagement."

General Steel faced the President. "We can direct our fighters to harass the Soviet flight in an attempt to stop them or alter their course. If that doesn't work, do we have your permission to intercept them? Can we open fire first?"

Apprehension clouded the face of Allan Steiner. After a moment, he shook his head firmly. "No, we will *not* initiate a hostile act. We will harass them only."

Both generals stiffened. Morrison blurted out, "Sir, we *must* intercept the Russians! There's no other way to stop them."

"Yes, there is," the former professor half-smiled at his generals. "We're going to invade Saudi Arabia *first.*"

Beach at ARAMCO

With the dim light of dawn, the air was already uncomfortably warm, and it assaulted the nostrils with a foul odor of processed petroleum. The salty waves lapping at the coarse sand of the beach were too tepid to enter comfortably, though some beach-goers—who didn't mind the greasy water—would splash it on themselves for its evaporative cooling effect. The ARAMCO beach was one of the least attractive in Saudi Arabia, yet Americans and other Westerners considered it one of the best. The beach was the *only* one in the country where a woman could safely wear an ordinary bathing suit . . . providing she kept a long robe handy in case a Saudi showed up.

Spreading their blanket, the Swedish brunette spoke in a slight British accent. "Can we rest a while before jogging, Tom? I've been on my feet the last eight hours."

"I thought nurses read books during night shifts."

"That's at ordinary hospitals." She dropped to her knees on the blanket, stretched out face down, and sighed. "Believe me, *no* hospital in this country is ordinary."

Tom sat beside her and began massaging her back. "What kept you busy?"

"*Thirty-nine* emergency trauma victims."

"What from?"

"Arab drivers," she replied. "Wrecking their cars is about the only form of entertainment they have."

Sandi lay silently on the blanket. She lazily closed her eyes. As the shimmering sphere of the sun lifted above the horizon, its blinding reflection off the dark green Persian Gulf forced Tom to look aside.

He bent over to whisper in her ear. "Sandi, you're missing the sunrise."

She smiled. "I can feel it." The air was suddenly warmer by five degrees.

Lightly tugging at the ties of her string bikini, he asked: "May I?"

"Are you a gentleman?" she teased.

"An officer *and* a gentleman."

"Did you see the movie?"

"Nope."

"Well, he wasn't a gentleman anymore than you are."

"Fine," Tom good-naturedly replied, "you can *have* an oily suit."

"Oh, go ahead." Her voice was genial. She knew what was coming.

He shifted to a kneeling position at the head of her body and unhooked the bikini top. After brushing the long dark brown hair off her shoulders and pouring lotion into his palms, Tom leaned over to nuzzle the nape of her neck. His heavy hands slid effortlessly down each side of her backbone. Though her five-foot-nine frame carried an extra ten pounds, Sandi's statuesque figure normally halted conversation among members of the opposite sex when she entered a room—especially when riding on high heels. Tom's hands parted at her waist and curled around her full hips. He pulled at the sides of her body as his hands returned toward her shoulders.

"Tom," said Sandi wistfully, "when are you leaving?"

"When you've had all you can handle?"

She paused. "Isn't it the other way around?"

"What does that mean?"

"You Marines always retreat after taking your pleasure."

He ignored the gibe. "I thought you were talking about right now. I don't intend to leave off massaging you until you're *in pure ecstasy.*"

"I think you're getting more pleasure out of this than I am," she countered, enjoying his strong hands immensely but determined to keep the fact from him.

"Patience, my lady," he soothed. "Give it time."

Tom Hemingway was known by his military superiors as meticulous, hard-working, and brilliant—a natural leader by his own example. The Marine in him also knew the unreasonable demands an active military career could place on a family, which explained his consistent bachelorhood since being commissioned. The lack of one woman in his life had greatly enhanced his knowledge of all women, given the variety his lifestyle permitted.

He'd become particularly adept at giving small

pleasures to the ladies of his life, and they invariably reacted in the same manner—by falling in love. Hence, he'd also become an expert in watering the flames. Usually, the women were left confused if not unhappy . . . always with a hint of more to come, but never the full measure.

His standards for women were the same he used to appraise the men he led. The Marine pilots of his command were highly disciplined and carefully selected men, inherently blessed with unique physical and mental capacities. Few women he met compared.

Squirming into the blanket, Sandi asked, "How come a talented, 36-year-old like you isn't married?"

"There's a saying in the Corps," he recited pragmatically, "if the Marines wanted you to have a wife, they'd issue you one."

"We nurses have a saying, too," Sandi replied after a moment. "If a Marine's your date, a bed's your fate."

She twisted around to watch the little-boy smirk emerge on Tom's face. Her gaze was drawn to the broken pug-nose above his twisted smile, both the result of injuries received years earlier as a blocking fullback at The Citadel. His lips were too thick and the jaws too wide, yet this ruggedness attracted her, as it did most women. Her eyes dropped to take in the well-defined musculature beneath the thick hair of his upper body. Noticing her eyes, Tom sucked in his gut a bit more, rippling his shoulder and arm muscles as he did so. She smiled and replaced her head on the blanket. "So when are you leaving for the States?"

Damn, I hate that question, he mused, *even this time.* He considered asking his own question, but was uncertain how to phrase it.

"In three weeks."

"Well, easy come, easy go," she returned nonchalantly. He placed Sandi's arms tightly against her sides and crossed her legs. "Ready?" he asked. Without waiting for a reply, Tom twisted her feet at the ankles, neatly flipping Sandi onto her back.

"Hey, bozo," she protested good-naturedly. "The smorgasbord is uncovered."

It was his favorite sobriquet for her exposed anatomy. Grinning at the splendid sight, Tom poured a liberal portion of lotion across each breast and asked, "How's that?"

"You're crazy!" Sandi exclaimed in mock anger. She raised up on her elbows to stare at her glossy bosom.

Tom feigned innocence. "I thought you didn't want any oil on your suit."

She reclined again, actually relishing the freedom of her unfettered chest. "You're still crazy, Marine," Sandi repeated in a friendlier tone.

"Over you, babe," Tom replied softly. He began tracing her ribs, discreetly moving around the curves of her firm breasts, grazing them lightly only when necessary to obtain more lotion.

She arched herself as if reaching for his hands. "Are you crazy over me or my *body*, Tom?"

"What do you think?" he replied in a sardonic tone, then added, "It beats wrecking cars."

A slow grin crossed Sandi's face. "Are there any cars in the parking lot?"

Tom looked up and saw only her yellow Mustang convertible. "Nope, we're all alone."

She closed her eyes and Tom poured a circle of lotion around her navel, creating a small pool in its cleft. With one finger, he leisurely spread the lotion in ever-widening circles.

"Ummm," purred Sandi as he repeated the movement over and over until she was totally relaxed.

The woman now reclined before him had a taunting way. She appeared fond enough of Tom, but at the same time, Sandi kept her distance. She was sufficiently clever to restrict her display of affection for him—to maintain a mystery of her feelings, which only motivated a greater display of his feelings toward her in an effort to solicit the same.

It had become confusing for the Marine officer, accustomed as he was to working with the more straightforward minds of men. He knew, however, one thing for sure of this woman. Sandi possessed a trait he valued highly in his men. She had a head on her shoulders.

"Tree time," he announced. Lifting her right leg and hooking its heel to his shoulder, he dripped oil along its length, and eased both his hands down the leg . . . pausing to ruffle her thigh muscles. The second time Tom did this, she told him:

"You Marines know *all the right moves.*"

Stroking the leg several more times, he unhooked it and moved to the other one. As he finished the second leg, Sandi reached up to him with glazed eyes.

"Please, Tom."

Taking her hands, he resisted their downward

pull. When she opened pouting eyes, he falteringly spoke. "What . . . what do you think of marriage?"

Her eyes widened. Tom felt the tension release in her hands and added, "These last four months with you have been fantastic."

She paused to consider his meaning. "If that's a proposal"—she stopped for a negative reaction and, receiving none, continued—"my God, Tom . . . you haven't even said you loved me.

"Of course, I love you," he instantly declared.

Sandi looked askance. *"Of course, I love you,"* she repeated, mimicking his unemotional tone and rolling her eyes.

"When I get back to the States," he firmly stated, "I want you there waiting for me."

"Tom," she mildly remonstrated, "I'm not some corporal you can order around."

Confused by the direction his overture had taken, Tom selected what he considered a more direct approach. "Sandi, if I asked you to marry me, what would you say?"

Sandi smiled broadly. "I'd say that is the most bassackwards proposal I've ever heard of!" Seeing immediate hurt on his face, she gently added, "Why don't you ask and find out if you really want to know the answer?"

Realizing the folly in his plan to obtain her commitment first, Tom was even more uncertain of her reply. A noise from above blotted out his confused thoughts.

"Hey, we've got company!" yelled Sandi, searching for her bikini top.

Twelve hundred feet above, an AV-8B from

Tom's squadron floated down toward the two of them. Misnamed the ''Harrier'' by its British designers, the stout AV-8B's appearance was anything but that of its namesake—the slender, long-tailed English hawk. The aircraft's designers might have more aptly borrowed the name of their premier dogfighting breed—the bulky, square-jawed, pugnacious *bulldog*.

Like the canine, the AV-8B was a deadly opponent in close quarters. This superiority came from the four exhaust nozzles of its massive engine. Their direction could be adjusted inflight by the pilot. Normally, the nozzles were vectored (directed) aft as in conventional aircraft; however, within one second they could be vectored 98 degrees downward and forward to bring the plane to a near-instant hover. The nozzles could also be vectored to intermediate angles during air-to-air combat to increase turn rate and for rapid pitch/speed change. Experienced professionals often said the only plane that could outmaneuver a Harrier in a restricted airspace was another Harrier.

Cutting its power slightly, the Marine jump-jet began dropping in a near vertical descent. As it came closer, the roar of its powerful engine equalled that of a large passenger jet at takeoff.

Tom stood and defiantly waved the pilot away. Instead, the Harrier continued its descent. At 200 feet, the downward-deflected exhaust of the plane churned up a virtual sandstorm around the couple, and—having identified his commanding officer—the pilot increased power and ascended back over 1000 feet.

Tom glanced down at Sandi, who was sitting up

with her hands over her eyes in the settling powder. The well-oiled body was no longer visible. It now wore a thick coat of gritty, yellow sand.

Shaking his fist at the Harrier, Tom shouted, "You dumb sonofabitch!" He tried to make out the serial number on the aircraft's fuselage as its pilot hit his flare/chaff dispenser button. A gray canister jettisoned from a pod attached to the rear of the plane and tumbled to the beach.

Running to where the canister hit the sand, Tom opened it and found a small notebook. After reading its message, he jammed it into his waistband and bolted to the wet sand at the water's edge. With his foot, he spelled out:

SEND HELO ARAMCO HOSP

The Harrier pilot acknowledged by nodding his aircraft. The jet climbed away at a 45-degree angle.

Tom ran back to the blanket where Sandi now stood, hands on hips. "Look at me!" she stammered helplessly.

He attempted humor. "You're sandy."

"You're . . . you're . . ." she sputtered in frustrated rage. "Come on, let's go," Tom told her as he grabbed up their blanket and ice bucket. "I've got an Alert Three."

Sandi scoffed, "You have alerts twice a week."

"This is a *three,*" he emphasized. Tom grabbed her hand and pulled her toward the parking lot.

"Wait a minute!" she protested. "Let me wash the sand off first."

Tom paused all of two seconds. "We haven't got time," he snapped. At the car, he draped a blanket around Sandi and pushed her inside.

Fuming all the way to the hospital, Sandi finally

exclaimed: "Colonel, you want to know what I'd say if you asked me to marry you?"

He didn't invite the answer.

"I wouldn't marry a jarhead if he was the last man on earth!"

Over the Gulf of Oman

Captain Ken Carter, USN, wiped the sweaty palm of his right hand on his flightsuit, aggravated that he was freely perspiring in the coolness of the F-18 cockpit. A few minutes earlier, Carter had received instructions from the Constellation to overtake the Soviet flight, but when he'd requested his rules of engagement, Admiral Johnston had told him to stand by. As senior CAG (commander, carrier air group) of the airwings off the Constellation and Enterprise, Carter had overall command on the 48 F-18 Hornets chasing the Soviets.

"Falcon 101, this is Homeplate," came over his headset.

Recognizing the admiral's voice again, Carter replied, "I have you, Homeplate."

"Instructions for Red Dog flight are to harass and attempt to divert from Saudi Arabia. Do not open fire unless fired upon. Repeat: harass and attempt to divert, but do *not* initiate fire."

Carter tersely responded. "Clarify words: harass and divert."

Admiral Johnston knew the Soviets could be monitoring their transmissions and debated how to answer his flight commander. There had been no time to discuss these options before the F-18s were launched.

"Request clarification of instructions," repeated Carter.

"Buzz them. Thump them," offered the admiral. "Place your aircraft between the transports and runways if they try to land. Fly underneath if they prepare to drop paratroopers. Do anything you can. Just do not initiate fire."

"Anything we *do*," Carter suggested with obvious dissatisfaction, "could result in a firefight."

Admiral Johnston wanted to tell his CAG that he too was frustrated by the inadequacy of the orders from Washington. After a lengthy pause, he gave his final instructions. "Exercise your best judgment."

"Roger, Homeplate."

Carter remembered the last time he'd thumped another aircraft. It had been 23 years earlier, shortly after flight school. Coming from behind at high speed, he'd slipped beneath the other plane and swooped up directly in front of it. The resulting turbulence caused the other pilot to temporarily lose control of his aircraft. It was a game occasionally played by rookie pilots.

Due to a few isolated accidents, such aerobatics had been outlawed back in the early seventies. Knowing many of his younger pilots had never tried thumping another aircraft, Carter wondered if they could safely execute this maneuver now. He also knew an unplanned collision might appear deliberate to the Soviets.

Admiral Johnston's suggestion to have the F-18s position themselves beneath the Russian transports as they attempted to land didn't sound any better. Carter didn't relish ordering his fighter pilots to permit themselves to be sandwiched between the transports and runways. *That would be pure suicide,* he decided.

The White House

Wearing his perpetually pained expression, the slightly stooped figure of Secretary of State Clayton Walters hurried into the War Room. He was followed by Admiral Frank Sparks (Chief of Naval Operations) and General Edward Huering (Commandant of the Marine Corps). The President acknowledged their arrival by motioning them to the conference table where he was already seated with Steel, Morrison, and Hoolihan. After the JCS Chairman had provided a brief synopsis, the President spoke.

"From what I've been told so far, it's unlikely our military units in or near the Persian Gulf are sufficient to stop the Russian flight. Is that correct, Bob?"

"Basically," the JCS Chairman hesitated, "under—"

Cutting off the general, President Steiner continued. "Therefore, I recommend we invade Saudi Arabia . . . before the Soviets. If they think we've beat them to it, we may head them off. I doubt if they'll seek a direct confrontation with us."

"How?" Clayton Walters direly began, "can we invade Saudi Arabia within the next two hours?"

"Using 1800 Marines from one of our ships already in the Gulf," answered the President.

"Begging your pardon, sir," General Morrison dubiously commented. "We'll need a lot more than 1,800 men to invade and hold Saudi Arabia."

"Mr. President," interjected General Huering, "my Marines on the Puller are not your average soldiers. They're a Force Recon battalion—the elite of the elite, highly skilled in high-explosives, underwater tactics, guerrilla warfare, and airborne operations. They also possess our latest weaponry." The eyes of the bald-shaven Marine general challenged those of the other military men at the table as he added, "With their training and firepower, they can seize and effectively hold a substantial amount of territory."

"I hope you're correct, Commandant," said President Steiner gratefully, "but I don't intend to *hold* Saudi territory. We only have to temporarily appear to do so in the eyes of the Soviets. Now, does anyone have a better suggestion?"

The men at the table exchanged glances. When no one spoke up, General Steel said, "Mr. President, I concur with your idea. I'll draw up plans for your approval."

"You've got five minutes to draw them up," stated the President, who shifted his attention to Hoolihan. "Jim, get Derevenko on the hot line."

Hoolihan picked up the red phone at the center of the table and offered a skeptical hello. "Hello." Getting an immediate response, he said, "The President of the United States would like to speak to Premier Derevenko."

At the other end of the hot line, he heard words

spoken in an undertone and a second Russian came on the line. "This is the interpreter for Premier Derevenko. What do you wish to say?"

Hoolihan faced Allan Steiner. "Mr. President, his interpreter has asked for your message."

President Steiner frowned. "He doesn't *need* an interpreter." Before speaking into the phone, the President reached over to activate the speaker box on the conference table to enable others to hear the full conversation.

"This is the President of the United States. Tell Premier Derevenko only an ill-advised and foolish man could believe the United States would permit the invasion of Saudi Arabia."

The interpreter repeated the message in Russian, and President Steiner made a taut grin as he heard laughter and loud voices in the background . . . even before the interpreter had time to repeat his words. This told him the English-speaking Derevenko was also using a speaker box, and more important, his call had been expected.

"President Steiner," offered the interpreter, "we know nothing of an invasion of Saudi Arabia. It must—"

"Don't give me *that*!" interrupted the President. "Your flight from Afghanistan is with Soviet aircraft and Soviet pilots. We've observed them refueling."

After another background in Russian, the interpreter said, "Premier Derevenko asks me to tell you perhaps the Afghans are on a training mission."

"Only an idiot would expect me to accept that!" snapped the President. "We know your flight fought its way across Pakistani airspace." Allan Steiner stopped abruptly, awaiting a reaction to his remarks.

There was no laughter this time. Following a lengthy pause, the interpreter came back on the line. "The Premier of the Soviet Union suggests you have nothing to worry about. He wishes you a pleasant Good Friday."

"What's your name?" demanded the President of the interpreter.

"My name is Nikolai Vishinsky."

"Nikolai, give this message to your Premier with great care. The United States of America has *already invaded* Saudi Arabia. Within the hour, we will control the airport at Dhahran *and* the oil fields!" The President slammed the phone into its cradle.

When Hoolihan and Walters met eyes with Allan Steiner, they could see his fury was genuine, though it was also at himself. Still fuming, the President muttered, "Derevenko thought I'd just roll over and play dead, didn't he? Just because I wanted to cut the fat out of the defense budget."

For a moment he recalled his election platform of the previous year. After the Central American disasters, the voters had swung to their periodic anti-military stance, and he'd ridden it into the White House. Now, he wondered if his campaign rhetoric should have been more subtle? Had the Soviets taken his positions as signs of weakness to be exploited? He shook his head despairingly at the answers.

"Come on." The President nodded his head toward the Middle East wall grid where the Joint

Chiefs were congregated, indicating that Walters and Hoolihan should accompany him there.

"Gentlemen," the President told the military officers, "I've just told the Soviets we've invaded Saudi Arabia. Now, how quickly can we do it?"

"We've reduced it to three options," Steel replied. "Our forces can be split between Dhahran Air Base and the major oil fields lying directly to the south, or we can concentrate them at either the air base or the center of the oil fields."

"Which you do recommend, Bob?"

"I'd gamble the Soviet flight is headed for Dhahran," replied Steel without hesitation. "Whoever holds that air base will also control access to the major oil fields."

"What if you're wrong," suggested Clayton Walters, "and the Russian transports land or drop their 5000 men in the oil fields?"

"That's possible," nodded General Steel, "but they wouldn't last more than three to four days in the oil fields without logistical support, which would be nigh impossible unless they also controlled Dhahran Air Base. I might add it would be spreading our 1800 Marines rather thin if we were to distribute half or even all of them in the oil fields. To place the Marines in the oil fields effectively, we would have to accurately guess *precisely* where the Russians planned to concentrate their 5000-plus men . . . and I'm positive they'll be concentrated, wherever they're landed."

"What about Riyadh?" ventured Walters.

"The Saudi capital is two hundred miles into the interior," Steel promptly replied, "and of little tactical value."

A communications officer in the War Room handed Steel a memo which he read before repeating its message aloud.

"Satellite surveillance suggests two Soviet airborne divisions are poised at air base in Kandahar, Afghanistan for immediate deployment."

Steel handed the memo to the President. "Sir, *these* are the Russians who'll be headed for the oil fields."

President Steiner watched the flashing red dots on the wall grid a moment. Then he locked eyes with Steel. "Issue standby orders to send the Marines into Dhahran."

"Mr. President," began General Huering, "to quickly prove our intentions to Moscow, I'd suggest we precede the Marines with an aerial attack by the Harriers. The Soviets probably have people in there already who'll report our military actions back to Moscow."

"We could restrict the bombing to runways," Steel offered, to which the President readily nodded.

"In addition to a mock invasion," said the secretary of state, "may I suggest we call a press conference to announce our actions?"

General Morrison sourly injected, "That's not—"

"Excellent idea," cut in the President. "If we reveal our invasion to the world, Derevenko may *believe* us." He pivoted to Hoolihan. "Jim, call a press conference in ten minutes."

As the presidential assistant hurried out, General Steel exchanged glances with Morrison before speaking. "Mr. President, in 1985 the Saudis agreed to let us use their military bases in case of Soviet aggression, but *if you announce we're invading them,* we may have problems with their military."

The President smiled. "That's why I gave you standby orders, Bob. First, I've got to talk to King Asad and tell him to sit tight when we come in. While I'm doing that, why don't you notify the Puller of our plan." As the military men left the conference table, the secretary of state handed the President the receiver to a white telephone.

"We've had Ambassador Clark standing by," explained Clayton Walters. President Steiner took the phone and indicated Walters should switch the call to the speaker box.

"Ambassador Clark?"

"Yes, Mr. President."

"Is the king with you?"

"Yes, sir. He's in the communications center of the embassy with me."

"Good, I want my conversation with him taped."

"That's routine, Mr. President."

"I'd also like you to listen in."

"Just a moment sir." After a brief pause, Clark said, "We're both on the line."

"Asad, this is Allan. Has Ambassador Clark filled you in on the situation?"

"Yes," answered the king. "My air and land forces are on full alert. What are your plans?"

"We don't want to start World War III over this, Asad. So we've decided the best way to stop the Soviets is for U.S. military units to invade your country first."

For an instant the Saudi king froze. Dropping the phone, he barked an order to his Royal Guard officer who drew a pistol.

Clark saw the muzzle of the gun aimed directly at his head. He heard the hammer click back. "Mr. President! You *can't invade* Saudi Arabia!"

"Asad, you—" began the President.

"He's not listening anymore!" Clark blurted out.

"Tell him it's a *mock* invasion," said the President, "to throw the Soviets off."

"Your Majesty," implored Clark in a wavering voice, "it is *not* a real invasion!" He glanced at the leveled pistol and shivered as he added, "President Steiner only wants to fool the Russians."

Asad hissed another order and the red-bereted officer lowered his pistol. Recovering the phone, the Saudi king angrily declared, "Allan, you *cannot invade my country!* You must stop the Russians before they reach Saudi Arabia."

"That is not possible, Asad," began the President patiently. "The Soviets are over international waters, and they've taken no hostile actions toward military units of your country or mine."

"Then the Saudi air force will stop them," snapped the king.

"Asad, they may be bluffing . . . or testing us. If you attack them, you may give them the excuse they're looking for to invade your country."

The king's tone grew harsher. "If the United States declines to stop the Russians, then the Saudis will!"

Clayton Walters interjected, "Sir, may I speak to him?"

"Asad, my secretary of state wishes to speak to you." The President surrendered the phone.

"Your Majesty, I regret telling you this, but the aircraft in the Royal Saudi Air Force are no match for the Soviet planes."

The king paused a moment. "Then the land-based Hawk and Stinger missiles you have sold us for one billion dollars will stop the Russians, yes?"

"No, Your Majesty. These missiles will stop the Iranians, the Syrians, even the Israelis . . . but not the Russians. Their technology is superior to yours. It may even be better than our own."

The king fell silent as President Steiner took back the phone. "Asad, I have just been handed a communique from one of our AWACs over the Red Sea. I will read it to you.

A formation of 27 large aircraft have rendez-voused with 42 fighter-size aircraft at a point in South Yemen, 45 miles below the Saudi Arabia border. They have turned north, in the direction of Riyadh."

The President went on. "Do you remember who suppressed the South Yemen soldiers who remained loyal to their assassinated president in 1979?"

"Yes, I remember," replied Asad reluctantly. "Cubans . . . from Ethiopia."

"That's right, Asad. *Who* do you think are in those aircraft headed for Riyadh?"

The Saudi king groaned. "If my defenses are worthless against the Russians, what can I do?"

"Cooperate with me, Asad."

The king spoke in a subdued tone. "But you are a Jew, Allan. You are a Jew."

"That's ridiculous, Asad!" exploded the President after a stunned moment. "I'm only half—"

Allan Steiner knew it was useless to protest further. Though he had followed his father in becoming an elder of the Presbyterian church, it was far better known that his mother was born a Jew. And if bigots in his own country could hold it against him, certainly an Arab could. Now it was better to simply change the subject.

"Asad, do you *realize* your position at this moment? You are only one hour's flight-time from the concentration camps in South Yemen. The planes heading for Riyadh could take you and the 5000 other princes of your family back to those camps."

The king gave no response.

"Do you know who runs those camps, Asad? *East Germans.* How long do you think your family would survive?"

Still no response.

The President went on. "After the Marxists took over in Kabul, do you know how many Afghan civilians were listed by their regime as executed in the Poli Charki concentration camp? *Twenty-seven thousand!* Think of it—in a country with fewer people than yours."

President Steiner paused a few seconds. "Make your choice, Asad. And quickly!"

The king wearily replied, "You give me little choice."

"Not I," the President changed to a tight undertone. "It is *Derevenko* who gives you little choice. Listen to what I tell you now. Ambassador Clark,

take notes. Aircraft from our assault carrier, the
Puller, in the Gulf will simulate bombing attacks
on Dhahran Air Base within thirty minutes. We'll
also drop a few bombs on open runways of Riyadh's airport in case the Soviets have agents observing these airports. Then Marines off the Puller
will land at Dhahran.''

''I have a brigade of Pakistani commandos in the
eastern oil fields,'' countered Asad. *''They'' will come
to Dhahran instead of your Marines.''

''The Soviets would not hesitate to engage the
Pakistanis, Asad, but they'll think twice before taking on American Marines. And there is too little
time to transfer your men. My Marines are only
minutes away.''

''How soon will your Marines leave my country?'' Asad asked stiffly.

''As soon as the Soviet threat is gone.''

''I do not like your answer.''

President Steiner felt his position weakening.
''Asad, if we make a show of force, I believe the
Soviet threat will be discouraged . . . and the Mar-
ines will be back on their ship by nightfall.''

''That, I would like,'' affirmed the Saudi king.

''Then we have your permission, Asad?'' Hearing no reply, the President continued. ''And will
you notify your military commanders not to inter-
fere or respond to our actions?''

The American president waited for a reply this
time. It came falteringly and with obvious reluc-
tance.

''Yes, I will warn them . . . but I think you must
do more to stop the Russians.''

Allan Steiner was aware his predecessors had

tried for two decades to obtain Saudi permission to permit American military units on their soil. He considered whether to remind the king that American air force units, in fact, had been stationed at Dhahran Air Base at one time, but they had been asked to leave over a minor dispute. There was too little time for such discussion now, so he said instead, "We are. In a few minutes, I will hold a press conference to announce our invasion of your country. And I've already called Premier Derevenko to tell him the same. If these measures do not work, we will try to turn them back at Dhahran . . . without starting a war in which we would all lose."

"What of the planes coming from the south?" asked Asad. Temporarily at a loss, the President looked to General Steel before speaking. "Deploy your troops at the Riyadh airport." The JCS Chairman nodded in approval.

"We will do that."

"And Asad. Can you remain at the embassy? We may have to communicate again soon. I must leave now for the press conference. Good luck."

"Inshallah," the Saudi replied.

Replacing the receiver, President Steiner told General Steel, "Notify the Puller to execute their orders." As the President turned to leave, Clayton Walters stopped him.

"Sir, there are 40,000 American civilians in Saudi Arabia. Shouldn't we try to warn them what's happening?"

"Yes, of course. Instruct Ambassador Clark to do that."

"It won't be easy," Walters allowed.

"Why not?"

"No one's at work today, sir. It's Good Friday, and this is the Muslim holy day of the week."

"Tell Clark to do the best he can," the President ordered, "then join me at the press conference."

The President shook his head in disgust, recalling the first members of three Soviet airborne divisions had chosen *Christmas Eve* of 1979 to invade Afghanistan in order to install Babrak Karmal—who promptly issued a call to Moscow for troops which were already there.

"Before you leave, sir," said General Steel, "I'd like authorization to mobilize our Rapid Deployment Force in Europe, plus the Marine battalion with the Nimitz in the Mediterranean."

"You've got it."

Over the Red Sea

The Lear Jet was a private flight, one of hundreds flown each month from southern Europe. It cruised southward over the Red Sea at 31,000 feet, following an ancient trade route of smugglers from the Mediterranean to the population centers bordering the Red Sea. Modern-day runners of contraband called the route *the Riviera-Red Express* and used it primarily to transport highly prized but illicit items into Saudi Arabia. These included premium whiskeys and scotch, the highest-grade cocaine, adult video cassettes, and expensive Western women—preferably blondes.

The cargo of the Lear Jet differed in several respects from its usual contents. The American woman it carried was a redhead . . . and she was not bought.

Pulling herself upright on the sofa, she tossed her head to shake her sunstreaked auburn hair aside. A small, exquisite face gave her the appearance of a teenager, though she was nearing twenty-six. Her face was contorted with concern at the empty cockpit.

"Hamud . . . are you sure it's safe?"

"I've—" he smoothed his thick mustache while

47

debating whether Irene would prefer to believe she was the first.

"I'm sure it's been done many times," he assured her.

"Have *you* ever done it?"

He grinned impishly. "Never!"

"Liar," snickered Irene, pushing the Saudi prince back down onto the luxuriantly cushioned sofa.

Without rising again, Hamud reached a hand up and cautiously undid the lowest button of her blouse. She didn't move away or even notice the hand.

After checking the night sky through a window, Irene again shifted her attention to the empty cockpit of the Lear Jet, studying whether the aircraft was still level. Turning her head back to Hamud, she found his hand posed in mid-air . . . within the folds of her fully opened blouse.

The woman's eyes narrowed on his fingertips as they inched closer. She neither spoke nor moved—concentrating on the coming touch.

Noting her attentiveness, Hamud paused to let his fingers spread . . . suspending them over the pert breast.

As Irene took a deep breath, Hamud's bronzed face—dominated by the broad hook nose of the Saud family—took a raffish bent. His usually melancholy eyes sparkled at the game. One of the more westernized of the Saudi princes, he was known to expend prodigious sums gambling on the Riviera and entertaining beautiful women. But this one had remained unimpressed . . . even refusing the jewels other women eagerly sought. Therefore, she *amused* the Saudi prince, and now he chose to respond in kind.

"Never . . . never . . . have I seen such a magnificent rosebud."

In a trancelike state, Irene continued to gaze downward. His tone became official and mocking. "I, Hamud Abdul Aziz Al Saud pronounce you . . . my Nipple Queen."

"You turkey!" Irene cried out, the precious spell broken. Her long nails dug deep into his ribs as they rolled, giggling like children on the soft carpeted aisle.

Riyadh

The two Saudi military leaders stormed into the private office of Ambassador Clark in the American embassy. The haughty face of the six-foot-four Crown Prince displayed a neatly-sculptured black mustache and pointed beard. When excited, Saleem had a tendency to suck air between his brown, coffee-stained teeth, in addition to bouncing on the balls of his feet—an inherited mannerism accounting for his nickname: *the Royal Yoyo*. As commander of the Saudi national guard, Crown Prince Saleem led the 10,000-man private army of the ruling Saud family. His half-brother, Prince Rahman, followed him into Clark's office.

Rahman, 15 years younger and a few inches shorter than the 70-year-old Saleem, held the more powerful position of Minister of Defense and Aviation, because he was the first of King Abdul's 44 sons to pilot a jet. Rahman's bushy eyebrows arched delicately over soft, baleful eyes which furtively scanned the office's furnishings.

The king ordered his Royal Guard officer to close the door of the office as he stood to speak. "My brothers, a flight of Russian jets carrying 5000 men will arrive at our eastern border within two hours. And from South Yemen, another flight comes toward Riyadh. The Americans believe the planes from Yemen contain Cuban soldiers.''

"We must shoot the dogs down!" shrieked Saleem, bouncing already.

Accustomed to the outbursts of his half-brother, Asad waited a moment before continuing. ''We cannot do that,'' he calmly said.

''WE CAN!'' retorted Saleem, inhaling moistly through his teeth. ''WE MUST!''

''If we try,'' Asad looked to Rahman as he spoke, ''the Americans have said we will fail. They say our planes and missiles cannot stop the Russians.''

''Then why,'' Prince Rahman dourly asked, ''don't the Americans shoot them down?''

Asad made a hopeless shrug. ''The Americans refuse to attack first. They and the Russians are like two scorpions in a bottle. If one attacks, the second will strike back . . . and both will die. But if neither attacks, both live.''

''And then *we* shall die,'' sputtered Saleem.

Rahman pursed his lips in anguish. ''How shall we stop the planes from the south?''

"You're the defense minister,'' Asad reminded him. As this failed to solicit a response, the king continued. ''The Americans suggest we place our soldiers and missiles at the airport.''

''What of the oil fields?'' demanded Saleem.

The king shot a nervous glance at Saleem and continued to direct his words to Rahman. ''To discourage the Russians from landing in the east, the Americans propose to carry out fake attacks at the airports of Dhahran and Riyadh.'' Asad delicately cleared his throat. ''Then the Americans will pretend to invade Dhahran before the Russians. If they are first to occupy the air base, they believe the Russians will turn back.''

"The Americans are *no better* than the Russians!'' Saleem spit out. "Do you forget how they plundered our oil before 1973?''

"My brother,'' Asad said solemnly, "they have asked that we not oppose them.''

The Crown Prince sneered. "My men will *never* lay down their arms.''

"I cannot stop the Americans now,'' replied Asad faintly.

"*All* infidels must be opposed!'' declared Saleem. He glared a challenge at Prince Rahman.

"I shall send our planes east and south,'' asserted Rahman reluctantly, "to intercept the infidels.''

The king eyed his two brothers in acquiescence. "So be it.''

Hissing inwardly, Saleem said, "Let us kill Clark now and be done with him.''

Asad exchanged a brief, knowing glance with Rahman. They both knew the easily excited Saleem was ninety-nine percent bluster; nevertheless, it was an often-expressed wish of the king that he would outlive his appointed successor . . . for the sake of the kingdom.

"No,'' Rahman quickly countered, "now is not the time for that.''

"Our brother is right, Saleem,'' seconded Asad. "I must stay here to learn more of the American plans. Go now. Allah be with you.''

The two Saudi princes moved swiftly from the embassy as Asad left the office and entered an elevator to return to the communications center on the top floor of the embassy. At a console in this room, a stocky, 54-year-old man wearing the uniform of an Air Force major switched off the television monitor to the ambassador's office and looked up at Ambassador Clark. The lopsided grin and bright eyes of the uniformed man's face were the complete opposite of the somber image projected by most embassy operatives of the Central Intelligence Agency. Louis Fricke quipped, "So much for our Saudi *partners*."

Clark spoke calmly and deliberately. "Send a message to Washington informing them the Saudi leaders may not fully cooperate with our mock invasions. Include the fact that we're unable to contact American compounds because all telephone and telex lines are down. Then request permission to evacuate the embassy."

Just before the Saudi king entered, the first secretary of the embassy rushed in and approached the ambassador. He whispered to Clark, "The Royal Guard won't let me leave to warn our compounds."

"Why don't we send him in our helicopter?" Fricke suggested.

The ambassador considered the proposal and shook his head. "There's too little time now. We'll have to warn the compounds after we evacuate."

The White House

When the President entered the press room, it was not necessary to request those present to rise. At three hours before midnight in Washington, most members of the White House press corps were home with their families. Only eleven reporters were in the room, and they stood in front of the podium waiting.

At the rostrum, President Steiner made a brief smile. "Gentlemen and ladies of the press, I have but two minutes to announce what is likely to be the most important news of my presidency." He methodically enunciated his next words.

"Military units of the United States have intervened in Saudi Arabia."

Hands shot up among the reporters. "Mr. President! Mr. President!"

He extended a hand over the rostrum for silence. "Let me continue. We have intervened in Saudi Arabia to protect its strategic oil fields from the Iranian army . . . poised 300 miles to the north. According to our intelligence sources, the Iranians have orders to invade within 96 hours. The oil reserves of Saudi Arabia are vital not only to the United States, but also to our allies in Western Europe and the Far East. We will not permit Saudi

Arabia to suffer the same fate as Kuwait. Consequently, at the invitation of King Asad, within the last hour we have occupied the major military and oil installations in eastern Saudi Arabia.''

The President pointed to an upraised hand.

''Mr. President, how long will the United States maintain its forces in Saudi Arabia?'' asked Harry Kramer of the *New York Times*.

''Until that country is secure from external threats,'' replied the President.

UPI's George Epsen waved a hand. ''Mr. President, which units have you sent to Saudi Arabia?''

''Our Rapid Deployment Force in Europe and two Marine battalions.''

The President pointed to an unfamiliar reporter.

''Mr. President, Betty Dodds of the *Post*. Is this related to the violation of Pakistani airspace by planes out of Afghanistan just reported by Karachi?''

The President's inexperience at news conferences was as transparent as his deceptive reply. After too long a pause, he painfully offered, ''At this time, we know of no relationship between those aircraft and the Iranians.''

Hoolihan caught the eye of his embarrassed boss and motioned to his wristwatch.

''That's all for now,'' announced the President. He exited the room almost as quickly as the reporters, who raced down the double aisles to their phones. As the presidential party entered the elevator to return to the War Room, Hoolihan inquired, ''Mr. President, why didn't you tell them we were invading to head off the Russians?''

President Steiner knowingly looked to his secretary of state, who answered for him. "Jim, the reason the Soviets weren't mentioned is we don't want them to lose face in turning around."

"And the first rule of diplomacy," added the President, "is never challenge a fool any more than you have to."

Hoolihan debated whether the expression on the President's face was a smile or grimace. He decided the latter.

"Perhaps," continued the President, "it will give the Iranians something to think about, too."

When they re-entered the War Room, an aide offered a phone to the President. "Sir, Prime Minister Weimann of Israel wishes to speak with you."

President Steiner took the phone and sat at the conference table. "Hello, Mort."

"Greetings, Allan."

"Why are you calling?"

"We're curious why your Sixth Fleet gave us notice several of its helicopter squadrons would be flying over our airspace. Admiral Colby referred us to you."

"Mort, the Saudi king has requested that our military units enter his country to checkmate the Iranians in Kuwait."

Friendly sarcasm colored Weimann's reply. "The Iranians are *no* threat, Allan. Ninety percent of them are sick as a dog right now. Let us not play games. We know of the flights from South Yemen and Afghanistan. Do you need assistance?"

It occurred to Allan Steiner that the arsenal of the Israelis—the most powerful war machine in the Middle East—was the only military force in the area which *could* stop a serious Soviet thrust. Yet, he also knew the Israelis were the *only* people in the Middle East who could not be called upon. He stonily replied, "We have everything under control."

"Are you sure?" Weimann drew out.

Goddam . . . I wish I was mused the President, wrinkling an ear with a closed fist. "We'll let you know if we need anything."

"I've placed our National Defense Force on full alert just in case," offered Weimann.

"Thank you, Mort." After hanging up, the President addressed General Steel. "How soon can the Marines in the Mediterranean reach Dhahran?"

"If their choppers don't run into any problems refueling in northern Saudi Arabia," Steel replied, recalling the debacle experienced by the rescue helicopters in the aborted 1979 raid on Tehran, "they'll reach Dhahran in four to five hours."

"How quickly can they be on their way?"

"They're airborne, sir."

"Excellent," the President smiled. "Soviet satellites should have picked them up by now. How about the Rapid Deployment Force?"

Steel matter-of-factly replied, "It'll take four days to bring the RDF in."

"Four days?" President Steiner's tone was incredulous. "You've got to be kidding."

"No, sir. That's their time-frame. A light division requires four days to move that distance.

"Well," declared the President encouragingly, "let's bring in more transportation then."

"That's using every available aircraft, sir."

The President paused. "Does it include British military transports?"

Steel reluctantly admitted, "No, sir."

"French military transports?"

"No, sir."

"How about the planes Pan Am and TWA have in Europe?"

General Steel again replied in the negative.

"Then you're not utilizing *all available planes,* Bob."

"No, sir," responded Steel, "but—"

"No time for 'buts' now," interrupted President Steiner. He turned to Hoolihan. "Jim, get on the phone to Pan Am and TWA and alert them to our needs. Any problems . . . give me the phone."

Hoolihan inquired, "Where should I have them send their planes?" The President looked to the JCS Chairman.

"Rhein Main Air Force Base in Germany," replied Steel.

"Clayton," directed the President, "you get Paris and London on the phone. Explain the situation and tell them we need every military transport they can lend us."

General Morrison broke in. "Sir, this is highly irregular. We *can't* use those planes."

Thinking *that's your third strike, General,* President Steiner brusquely inquired, "Why not?"

The general raised his hands futilely. "It would break our security. It would tip off the Russians."

"That's exactly what we want to see happen, General," the President angrily retorted.

Morrison shook his head and half-turned away, then came back around and spoke with renewed urgency. "Mr. President, *we haven't even alerted Omaha yet.*"

President Steiner studied Morrison dispassionately. "Why do you want to alert Omaha?"

Morrison stared at his commander-in-chief as if the President was a complete idiot. "We've got to get the bombers in the air," the general exclaimed. "Before it's too late!"

"And what would that accomplish?" The President remained as placid as his tone.

Morrison paused in further disbelief. After glancing at the other JCS members, who had chosen to remain spectators to the exchange, the general forcefully replied, "It'll let the Soviets know *we mean business!*"

"Then," began the President impassively, "they'll put their strategic bombers in the air . . . right, General?"

"Yes, sir!" Morrison's face split into a wide grin, relieved he'd finally got his point across. "That's what is done in this type of situation."

President Steiner raised his voice. "General Morrison, I've told you before that's precisely what we *don't* want to see happen at this time."

Morrison gawked at the President. "Sir, you're violating *too many* military rules."

President Steiner waited a moment to calmly observe his antagonist. "I would prefer to violate your military rules, General . . . than violate world peace."

The general glared in repudiation.

Glowering back, the President harshly asked, "How long have you been on duty, General Morrison?"

It took a moment to register. "Since 0600 this morning," he replied.

The icy edge to President Steiner's voice halted all movement and talk in the War Room. *"Then it's time you went home, General."*

Morrison's blank expression went to bewilderment.

"Go home, General," repeated the President firmly. When the perplexed officer still did not move, President Steiner addressed the JCS Chairman. "Bob, have the Air Force Deputy Commander report to the War Room immediately . . . to relieve General Morrison."

Steel went to the speechless general, took his arm, and eased him from the room as a civilian rushed into the War Room and handed Clayton Walters an envelope. Before he'd completed the first sentence of the message inside, Walters began reading aloud.

"After observing Asad meet with Crown Prince Saleem and Prince Rahman at embassy, we are uncertain of their cooperation. Some opposition may be encountered. Unable to warn American compounds, as telephone and telex lines down. Request approval for embassy evacuation."

"That doesn't make sense!" the President exclaimed. *"Why* would Asad change his mind?"

"Mr. President," began Walters gravely, "the Arabs are masters of prevarication. They often say what they believe others wish to hear, and then do the exact opposite."

Allan Steiner nodded as he smirked, thinking the prevarication label might be aptly applied also to a few members of Congress. Clayton Walters interrupted his thoughts.

"I suggest we evacuate the embassy . . . before we lose control of the situation."

"Is that possible?" the President questioned. "With the king there?"

Walters nodded his head. "Most of Asad's guards are probably waiting outside the building. And this being a holiday, there should be fewer than 15 of our own people in the embassy. The embassy helicopter could do it in one trip."

"I didn't know we kept helicopters with that capacity at embassies," commented the President.

"Larger helicopters are at all Arab embassies, sir. They could go to the Lockheed compound or one of the other large enclaves of Westerners outside of Riyadh."

"Okay, order the evacuation," agreed the President. After a pause, he quickly added, "Tell Clark I'd like Asad to accompany them . . . for the king's own safety."

Walters was taken aback. "Shouldn't we let the Saudis protect him, sir?"

"That's who I was thinking of protecting him *from,* Clayton. I wouldn't put it past the Soviets to have a Quisling waiting in the wings."

Clayton Walters doubtfully eyed the President, who continued, "When you tell them to evacuate, instruct Clark to bring out a tape of the conversation I had with Asad, plus the one with his brothers if it exists." President Steiner turned to the JCS Chairman. "Bob, if there's sufficient time, have the Marines on the Puller notify all nearby American compounds of the Soviet flight and our response."

Riyadh

In his Defense Ministry office, Prince Rahman paused at the wide window overlooking the largest public square in the capital of Saudi Arabia. He frowned at the sight of scattered men in Western-style clothes, as their stilted movements broke the symmetry of the scores of Saudis gracefully gliding in their thobes (cotton shifts) across the plaza for early morning prayers. It also annoyed the prince when foreigners referred to this plaza as "Chop Square" instead of its proper name: the Dira.

Rahman sat at his desk and tapped out a code on a console built into the desk-top. Swiveling around, he watched a panel in the cabinet behind his desk silently slide sideways, revealing a medium-frequency two-way radio. After tuning it to 2485 kilohertz, Rahman spoke into its microphone.

"Come in, Fox One."

A computer voice instantly responded, *"Call being routed."* A few seconds later, a man's voice came up. "This is Fox One."

"This is the Lion," responded Rahman. "I have sent my planes to intercept the Russian flights. My land forces will continue to guard the northern frontier and the oil fields. They will not oppose your Marines at Dhahran."

Fox One urgently asked, "Can you control the national guard in the Eastern Province?"

"Maybe," Rahman cautiously replied, "in some areas."

"You must control *all* Saudi military forces in the east."

"That is not possible," Rahman insisted. He knew even the Crown Prince could not fully control some of the Bedouin chieftains among the national guard units.

The voice on the radio became harsh. "Then *make it possible!* This could be the opportunity you've been waiting for."

Rahman paused to consider the prospects and quietly replied, "I will try."

"Why don't you tell The Yoyo to stay in Riyadh where his men can protect the royal family?"

"I will try," repeated Rahman with only slightly more fervor.

"Good. Contact me with any news, and remember," stated Fox One firmly, "do not make mistakes . . . like your brothers."

Over the Persian Gulf

As his fighters passed over the Strait of Hormuz, Captain Carter watched the gray morning haze below take on a reddish-brown hue as they entered the befouled air of the Persian Gulf.

Two hundred thirty miles to the northwest, Jim Toomey, the air control officer of a U.S. Navy E-2C out of Oman, grinned in relief. The F-18s finally had come in range of the revolving radome (a 24-foot-wide disc) mounted on a pylon above the fuselage of his twin-prop electronic surveillance aircraft.

The display panel of Commander Toomey's microcomputer printed out:

Red Dog flight is on 310 radial of Hornets. Hornets will overtake in 6 minutes. Red Dog in tight formation at 22K.

Toomey hit the orange button on his console and the printout on the display panel was instantly garbled, relayed to the airdata computer of Captain Carter's F-18, and degarbled. Carter's display panel lit up and the printout appeared in its original form. The entire transmission had required less than two seconds.

Captain Carter scanned the message twice before electronically acknowledging its receipt. *What the hell am I going to do?* pondered Carter. No further directions had come from the Constellation. It had been 18 years since he'd taken a fighter aircraft into combat; and even then, the restrictions hadn't been this bad. A glimpse at his fuel gauge told him the F-18s wouldn't make Dhahran at the rate they were burning fuel. It occurred to Carter that he might not return from the mission. For a second, he thought of Anita . . . his parents . . . playing ball in college . . . making it through flight school. The solution came.

Carter punched his UHF button. "Strike Force, this is Falcon 101. Descend to 21K."

As the F-18 formation descended, Carter partially described his plan. "We close in five minutes. When Ilyushins are sighted, I will designate sectors to squadron commanders who will assign an F-18 escort to each transport. Confirm to me when match-ups complete. On my command, we will then assume the same flight formation as the Ilyushins. When both formations coincide, again on my command, escorts will move behind and under the bellies of Ilyushins, maintaining a 500-foot interval. Further instructions to follow."

A few seconds later, Carter decided what to do with the two extra F-18s in each squadron and punched his UHF button. "Strike Force, this is Falcon 101. The following modifies previous. Each squadron commander will assign his two least-experienced pilots to fly CAP with me at 24K. Their mission will be to respond to any hostile fire."

One of his squadron commanders promptly came

up on the UHF radio. "Falcon 101, did you say
'least-experienced' pilots?"

"Affirmative," replied Carter. "The *two least-experienced pilots* in each squadron will fly CAP."

Carter mused, I hope Ivan is listening. This in
mind, he hit his UHF button. "Strike Force, this
is Falcon 101. Under no circumstance do we fire at
Red Dog flight . . . unless they fire *first*. I repeat,
do not fire unless fired upon. Squadron commanders, acknowledge my last."

"Roger 101," repeated four times.

Checking his fuel gauge again, Carter calculated
he had less than 19 minutes of remaining fuel. His
display panel lit up with a second message from the
E-2C.

*38 F-15s—Saudi Royal Air Force—approaching head-
on intercept with Red Dog. Close three minutes.*

Captain Carter swore to himself. He knew the
Saudi fighter jockeys would be ineffective against
the Fulcrums, but they might be effective in delaying his own plan—beyond the ability of his flight's
remaining fuel.

Ten seconds later (after the radome of the E-2C
had completed another full revolution), more data
appeared on Carter's display panel.

*10 Fulcrums from Red Dog moving out to intercept
F-15s. Mach II speed. Close 70 seconds.*

After electronically confirming the identity of the
hostile aircraft headed in his direction, Colonel Tupolov spoke into his headset. "Assume file forma-

tion . . . with 100-meter stepdown at 200-meter intervals.''

The ten Fulcrums neatly tucked themselves in a slanted file behind their commander, who then barked his next order. ''Prepare program fire-control computers for tandem execution.'' A few seconds later, Tupolov ordered, ''Count off,'' starting with himself. This permitted his pilots to combine their computers into a single unit which would select separate targets among the oncoming aircraft. The count reached ten, and Tupolov completed his instructions.

''Execute Immelman after release. I will commence fire in six seconds. Five, four, three, two, one.'' Releasing four missiles, Tupolov jammed his throttle forward, forcing his aircraft into a steep, backward-curling climb. As his Fulcrum began to assume an upside-down position, he smoothly righted it and headed back to rejoin the Ilyushins.

Each of the other Soviet fighters duplicated the actions of their leader.

Commander Toomey punched the orange button to relay the latest computer message to the flight leader of the F-18s.

Fulcrums released missiles. Missile speed indicates Sparrow class. Fulcrums returning to Red Dog flight.

Toomey impatiently waited ten seconds for the radome to revolve 360 degrees and register the results of the missile release. He started to count and looked down at his display panel after the required time had elapsed. No message appeared. *Did they miss?* he thought. *They couldn't have.* He counted out the interminable seconds of another revolution of the radome.

In his F-18, Carter wondered if the Saudis were close enough and smart enough to release their own missiles.

"Damn," Toomey exclaimed in an extended breath as he read his display panel.

Two F-15s remain of Saudi flight. They have made 180-degree turn.

After receiving this last message from the E-2C, Carter began having serious doubts whether his plan would work. And his fuel gauge showed only 14 minutes of remaining fuel.

U.S.S. Puller
in the Persian Gulf

Having received his orders from Colonel Moore, the overall commander of the Marine Amphibious Unit (MAU) on the Puller, Lieutenant Colonel Thomas E. Hemingway now stood before his pilots.

"Listen up!" he snapped.

The strident words silenced the wardroom chatter and the seated men focused their attention on the five-foot-ten, broadshouldered commander of the Puller's composite air squadron. Hemingway tensed as he spoke, and the bulging biceps of his black-haired arms strained at the rolled-up sleeves of his flightsuit. His build and dense body hair had led to the running name of *Gorilla* among his peers. As was his habit when initially speaking, Hemingway spoke in a low voice, forcing his listeners to strain forward in order to make out his words. It was his way of getting complete attention.

"Recon's loading up in our Stallions because there's a flight of Commies coming up the Gulf from the Indian Ocean. It's codenamed 'Red Dog' and includes 40 Ilyushins and 53 MiG-29s. Higher-up says their objective could be the air base at Dhahran. If so, they'll be passing over our position in 85 minutes. Another Soviet flight from South Yemen is headed toward Riyadh.''

Hemingway surveyed the immobile faces before him. They were frozen, as if in a still photograph. He continued.

''Our mission comes directly from JCS. We're to simulate aerial attacks on Riyadh's airport and Dhahran Air Base. Then we're to support Recon in defending Dhahran. JCS thinks the Commies will turn around if we already occupy it. Harriers will drop two loads of MK-81s on open runways of Dhahran and return to saddle up Sidewinders. The Saudi military units on the base have been briefed. Stallions will commence immediate transfer of Recon to the air base. The second wave of Stallions will offload as much combat gear as possible from the ship, then go under the tactical control of the ground commander, Colonel Banks. Recon's immediate objectives are the Control Tower and fuel dumps in the northeastern sector of the base. Any questions from the Stallion pilots?''

There were none. Hemingway checked his watch.

''I want the first Stallions and support helos airborne in five minutes,'' he growled. ''Move out!''

The helicopter pilots cleared out of the wardroom, leaving only the Harrier pilots in the high-backed easy chairs. Each of them feigned a nonchalance that none of them felt. As Hemingway exchanged glances with his pilots, a flicker of a smile played on some of their faces.

''Don't get your hopes up,'' he told them. ''I don't know if we're going duckshooting this morning or not. The Hornets on the Connie and Big E

were ordered to harass and divert the Russians . . .
whatever that means. If the F-18s don't stop them,
we're to meet them with Sidewinders, but we're
not to open fire unless they fire first.''

Seeing grimaces coming up, Hemingway added,
''Yeah, I know these are mucked-up orders.''

Captain ''Potato Joe'' Graybeal flashed his hand.
''Colonel, are we going to *have time* to deliver two
loads of MK-81s?''

''What're you getting at?''

''Even with two loads, we're not going to crater
more than three miles of runway. There's still nine
more miles at Dhahran.''

Hemingway stroked his chin. ''You're right . . .
the bombs are for show anyway. We'll drop one
load and pick up Sidewinders.''

''Dammit, I almost forgot,'' continued Hemingway, shaking his head, ''We're supposed to warn
American compounds what's happening, too.'' He
looked to Graybeal.

''Joe, you're going to Riyadh. Have your plane
fitted with two MK-81s and four Sidewinders, plus
fuel pods. Drop the bombs on the Riyadh runways
within sight of their Control Tower. Before you
launch, get the locations of the American com
pounds in Riyadh from CIC and do what you can
to alert them.''

''Want me to mess with the planes from South
Yemen?'' Graybeal eagerly asked.

''No! They'll be well-escorted. Stick to the
American compounds.'' Hemingway jerked a
thumb toward the hatch of the wardroom. ''Get
going! You're going to need full throttle to get there
in time.''

Hemingway addressed the remaining pilots. "When you return for Sidewinders, CIC will give you assignments to warn the compounds. I'm going directly to ARAMCO after unloading my bombs. At 0530 hours, we'll marshall at 15K over the Dhahran Control Tower. Let's go!"

Riyadh

A phalanx of 60 Bedouin, each man over six feet tall and wearing the distinctive red-and-white checkered gutra (headdress) of the Saudi national guard, bustled into the white, unimposing two-story building of the only television station in Riyadh. The humble edifice of Riyadh TV was in marked contrast to the grand architecture of the city's other public buildings—perhaps testimony to the omnipotence of the Saudi religious leaders, who had vehemently fought the late King Faisal for years before tolerating the introduction of the "infidel's" television to Saudi Arabia.

Following closely behind the guardsmen was their commander, Crown Prince Saleem. The Bedouin muddled menacingly in the hallways until Saleem led them into the small room which served as the studio of the station. One of the guard officers brought a short, bespectacled Egyptian before Saleem.

"Your Highness, this is the station manager."

The Crown Prince scowled at the timid Egyptian before exclaiming in his high-pitched voice, "I shall make an announcement at once on the television."

"Your Highness," the manager meekly offered, "that is not possible."

"Seize him!" shrieked the affronted prince.

Two Bedouin flanked the Egyptian and grabbed his arms, raising him off his feet. As the terrified man gaped at Saleem's khanjar (dagger) sliding from its sheath, he struggled to make his voice audible.

"The prayers . . . Your Highness, the morning prayers." The Egyptian's eyes pointed to the clock on the studio wall. The long narrow second hand of the clock was on the upswing, 15 seconds from 5 A.M.

The two guardsmen instantly released their grip and the Egyptian collapsed to the floor. Glaring at the clock, Saleem snapped, "Let us *pray,* then!"

A wizened imam who had silently observed the proceedings from a corner of the studio came forward. Getting to his feet, the station manager joined the imam before the standing microphone on a short dais. Raising his hand as he watched the clock, the manager signaled his director in the control room. The imam began to recite from the Koran as the Egyptian moved out of camera range and dropped to his knees.

A few guardsmen kneeled with the manager, and within seconds all in the room were on their knees.

Concluding five minutes of prayer, the imam hastened from the studio and the station manager cautiously approached Saleem.

"Your Highness, we—"

The Crown Prince silenced the Egyptian with a wave of his hand and strode to the microphone where he pointed to the control room. "Let them begin," he ordered.

The station manager nodded to his director.

The still-smoldering prince shouted into the microphone as he would before a multitude, forcing rapid adjustments in the control room. "In the name of Allah, the Compassionate, the Merciful, heed my words! The kingdom is being attacked by infidels. As I speak, their airplanes are crossing our sacred borders. We must oppose the foreigners . . . *wherever we find them!* In the name of Allah, *death to the infidels!*"

Saleem drew his khanjar and with each chant— "Death to the infidels!"—he thrust the curved tip of the blade higher until he was joined by his guardsmen and the building reverberated with their fervor. When he'd howled himself hoarse, the Crown Prince stepped down from the dais and beckoned the Egyptian before him.

"You will repeat my words *every ten minutes!* Do you understand?"

The station manager bowed low. "It will be done, Your Highness."

Saleem and his men stalked from the building.

A short while later, an agitated mob of several thousand Saudi men surrounded the Riyadh TV building. They were held back by members of the national guard, left there by Saleem to ensure the station followed his instructions.

Over the Persian Gulf

Finishing the message on the computer display, Captain Carter consciously loosened his grip on the Hornet's throttle. *Lighten up* he told himself *for the fine touch*. The thought took him back to his last dogfight over Haiphong. He scanned the display again.

24 Fulcrums separated from Red Dog flight. Headed toward Hornets. Coming in at three o'clock.

He relayed this data to his squadron commanders and spotted the Russian fighters forty seconds later swinging around in a wide arc to take up positions directly behind his F-18s at a half-mile interval. Carter was much relieved a few minutes later when he made visual contact with the main Soviet flight and no fireworks had broken out. The Ilyushins offered *safety,* at least from the Fulcrums' missiles. Now the Russians would be foolish to release any missiles at the F-18s, as the Hornet pilots could easily dodge most of them, leaving the Ilyushin engines to suck up the errant rockets. The American commander spread his F-18 squadrons to generally conform with the Ilyushin formation before telling them, "Strike Force, commence matchup."

Carter repeatedly checked his chronometer as his squadron commanders matched their pilots to the Russian transports. When the formations finally coincided, the F-18s started moving into stepdown positions to their respective Ilyushins. As they did so, Colonel Tupolov ordered a Fulcrum into a shorter stepdown to each of the threatening Hornets.

Seeing no interference to his plan yet, Carter hit his UHF button. "Strike Force—on my command—climb and take up position thirty yards to left-front of your Ilyushins. Accomplish this in *twenty seconds*. Execute!"

As the forty American fighters ascended in unison, the computer voice of Carter's F-18 announced, *"Bingo! Bingo!"* His fuel was now critically low.

Tupolov warned his transports, "Comrades, the Americans approach you from below. Maintain your speed and direction. *Do not* let them alter your course!" To himself, the Russian commander thought *whatever you Americans do, you will do it only once.*

At the relatively slow speed of the F-18s, the air turbulence experienced by the transports was minimal. Carter prayed he was guessing the right distance as his thumb depressed the UHF button. If it was too far, there wouldn't be fuel for a second try; if too close, each of the transports would break up in a terrifying conflagration.

"Strike Force—on my command—close to fifteen yards directly in front of their canopies. You have ten seconds. Execute!"

A communications technician in one of the Russian transports told his superior, "Lieutenant, the American fighters are to close within fifteen meters of our cockpits!" This was relayed to Tupolov who quickly repeated his previous orders to the Ilyushin pilots as Carter issued his final command.

"Strike Force"—the American commander took a deep breath—*"hit your afterburners!"*

From the side-by-side twin exhausts of each Hornet, a six-foot-wide mass of white-hot flame emerged as their powerful engines went to maximum throttle. The effect on the Ilyushin cockpits was immediate. The thermal-shock cracked and crazed the surface of the canopies into a fine spiderweb network that obliterated the vision of the pilots within. From a distance, the canopies appeared to have frosted over.

Within seconds, the F-18 Hornets rocketed a mile in front of the Russian formation. The trailing MiGs also shot forward in pursuit, a few of them having to dodge Ilyushins that were drifting as their pilots could no longer see to maintain their flight formations.

"Come back, you idiots!" shrieked the enraged Tupolov at the pursuing MiGs. "Forget the Americans!"

By hastily instructing the squadron commanders of his MiGs in a sequence similar to that used by the American flight leader, Tupolov re-established control of his transports. Using visual communication through the tail-gunners of the Ilyushins, the MiG pilots guided their respective transport pilots until separate radio frequencies could be assigned to each pair of aircraft.

"Those whoring bastards," swore Tupolov, realizing he now had unrestricted use of only twelve Fulcrums, not including his own. Having no alternate instructions, he maintained his formation on course, intending to follow his orders explicitly.

Carter keyed his mike. "Homeplate, this is Falcon 101. Have used afterburners to roast canopies of Ilyushins. They are now flying blind. Our fuel levels too low to continue. Request instructions."

Johnston's response from the Constellation came instantly.

"This is Homeplate. We have approval to land in Oman . . . at Misirah Air Base. Look for long wide valley near tip Musandam Peninsula. Great flying! Repeat: Great flying!"

Carter punched his UHF button. "Strike Force, this is Falcon 101. Follow me on bearing 174. We will try to make air base at northern tip of land mass to south. If you cannot make it, eject over land as close as possible to coast."

ARAMCO Compound

"Come on, Dori. Pitch!" yelled Kevin.

The softball was suspended in midswing as his twin sister froze. She looked over her right shoulder. The muffled thunder of explosions in the direction of Dhahran Air Base had diverted her attention.

"Let's play ball!" implored Kevin. "That's just another Saudi hot dog bailing out."

It was not unusual for residents of ARAMCO (the largest compound for Westerners and non-Saudi Arabs in the country) to hear fighters of the Royal Saudi Air Force slamming into the terrain of the air base. Few of the pilots lost their lives in these crashes, as they were quick to yank their ejection handles—a far easier maneuver than attempting to regain control of their planes. The air base was littered with the charred remains of these aircraft, many of them tail up with their noses embedded deep in sand.

Dori flung the ball, and her 12-year-old brother swung hard. Missing completely, his body contorted in a twist.

"Hey, Elmer Fudd!" taunted his sister, using the nickname he hated. "You swing like an old cow."

On the next pitch, Kevin controlled his swing and smacked a line drive directly at his tormentor. She ducked, pushing her glove out at the projectile. When ball and glove both fell to the ground, Dori snapped up the ball and threw out her brother.

As Kevin rounded first on his way to the outfield, his attention was drawn to a noisy, gray and olive-green camouflaged aircraft overhead. He slowed to a walk, then stood still, craning his neck upward. The Harrier maintained a near-level flight position as it descended in a deep slant to the ground, much like a bird preparing to alight.

"What kind of plane is that?" shouted Kevin. "It looks like it's going to crash."

The boy got no reply as the screaming whine of the dropping aircraft drowned out his voice. Its exhaust nozzles were almost vertical at 70 degrees as Colonel Hemingway aligned his slightly nose-up plane with the street bordering the playing field. At 15 feet, the Harrier made a familiar wobble when he increased power, slowing the plane considerably for touch down. His wheels hit the concrete with a jolt and the plane landed at a speed of 38 knots. The roar of his engine fell away as Hemingway brought it to idle and rotated his nozzles aft. Applying his brakes, he gently brought the plane to a rolling stop within ninety yards.

After letting his engine whine down, Hemingway popped his canopy and climbed out of the cockpit. The children, having recognized the stars-and-bars insignia on the side of the fuselage, ran to greet him. As they crowded around the pilot; he forced a smile. "What're you kids doing playing softball this early?"

"We have to play now," Kevin answered. "By seven, it's too hot."

Hemingway started to say, "The Russians are coming," and thought better. He pointed to a cluster of ranch-style homes several hundred yards away. "You kids live over there?"

"I do," nodded one of the children.

"Me, too," responded Kevin and Dori simultaneously—a trait the redheaded twins often displayed.

"You kids come with me," ordered the pilot as he began running toward the homes. Most of the children hopped on bikes, easily keeping pace with the pilot. At the first home, Hemingway paused to knock loudly at its open door before rushing inside.

"What's he doing?" asked Kevin of no one in particular.

"I think *I know*," responded Dori in a low voice.

"What?" inquired one of the children.

"What do you *think* he's doing?" Dori said with a knowing smile. The others looked at her quizzically.

"Dummies!" she finally exclaimed. "He's going to the bathroom."

A few giggled at the suggestion as the frowning pilot came out the door. "No one's home," he gruffly remarked. *"Who* has some parents who are at home?"

Surprised and frightened by the pilot's new tone, no one responded.

"Come on, kids," Hemingway pleaded forcefully. "I've got to talk to an adult."

Dori hesitantly spoke. "They're at the services."

"Services?" queried the pilot.

"You know . . . church," Dori replied.

"How far is it from here?"

Kevin pointed up a street. "Two blocks that way and to the left." It was considerably farther than the first house had been from the ball diamond.

"Well, take me there *quick!*" Hemingway demanded. He studied Kevin's dirtbike a moment. "Son, can I borrow your bike?"

The boy pushed his bike forward, and Hemingway straddled it as Kevin hitched a ride on another one. A few of the kids raced ahead of the pilot who at first awkwardly peddled the small bicycle. When they reached the end of the left-hand street, Hemingway stopped at the house where some of the children were already waiting. Except for its color, the home resembled the others on the street.

"This isn't a church," Hemingway stated as he dismounted.

"They don't allow churches," replied Dori breathlessly beside him. Hemingway looked down at the slender, heavily-freckled girl.

"The Saudis," she explained.

As the door was also open to this house, Hemingway hurried inside without knocking. Entering a hallway, he found adults seated in a broad living room and adjoining veranda. Coming into the room, the Marine pilot stood silently among bowed heads as a short, middle-aged woman in a white, flowered dress read from a small Bible.

". . . are those who mourn, for they shall be comforted. Blessed are the meek, for they shall inherit the earth. Blessed are those who hunger and thirst for righteousness, for they shall—"

"Excuse me!" Hemingway interrupted.

The woman stopped reading and everyone turned to stare at the intruder, behind whom the children had gathered.

"You're being"—Hemingway hesitated, searching for the right words—*"invaded."*

"Yes," smiled the woman, "we can see that. Would you like to join us?" Hemingway darkly frowned at the light laughter and the kind faces. His voice was dead serious.

"The *Russians* are invading Saudi Arabia. I'm Colonel Hemingway, with the Marines on the U.S.S. Puller in the Persian Gulf. My forces have already occupied Dhahran Air Base."

The Marine took scant satisfaction as his words wiped the smiles off the friendly faces. "I have instructions to warn as many of the American compounds in this area as possible. I suggest you remain inside ARAMCO until you hear otherwise."

Most of the adults were now standing. One of them asked, "Where've the Russians landed?"

"They haven't yet. We're expecting them to come into Dhahran. That's all I can tell you. I have to go now." Hemingway abruptly pivoted and was halfway down the hallway before he paused. Turning around, he spoke to the nearest adult. "Tell everyone to start phoning their friends in ARAMCO and other compounds . . . to warn them also."

"We can't" replied the man. "The phones are down."

"Damn," said Hemingway under his breath.

"I've got a ham radio," offered a girl's voice behind them.

The two men scrutinized the slim girl, who unfalteringly returned their gaze. "A lot of other compounds have hams, too," said Dori. "I know most of their call signs."

"What's your name, young lady?" asked Hemingway.

"Dori . . . Dori Norlin."

"And yours?" Hemingway inquired of the man.

"I'm her father. Name's John."

"Great," said Hemingway. "Use your radio then." Rushing from the house, he ran to the dirtbikes in the driveway and picked out the one he'd ridden earlier. The pilot looked back to the door of the house, but Kevin was already beside him.

"I need your bike again, son."

"Sure, mister. I'll run beside you."

This time, Hemingway arrived at their destination first, slightly ahead of the boy. Placing the bike behind the backstop, he sprinted to the Harrier and climbed into its cockpit. Before closing his canopy, he checked the clearance of his aircraft and saw Kevin standing no more than 50 feet away. Hemingway motioned the boy over to him.

"Get behind the backstop," yelled the pilot. "My exhaust is going to kick up a lot of dirt and rocks."

As the boy ran to the backstop, Hemingway slid his canopy shut and hit the start button. At first there was a low whining noise from behind the cockpit. The whine retarded a moment and then exploded in a deafening roar as the engine fired. Conducting his instrument check during the minute it took to bring up his engine, Hemingway hurriedly connected his oxygen supply, pressure system to inflate his G-suit in tight turns, and a survival pack (dinghy and life vest). After fastening leg restraints in case he needed to eject, Hemingway strapped himself to four more pairs of harnesses before attaching oxygen and radio leads to his flight helmet.

Adjusting the exhaust nozzles of the Harrier ten degrees from the horizontal, Hemingway glanced at the backstop. Kevin stood behind it, hands tightly covering his ears.

The pilot applied his brakes and brought the throttle to 55 percent. After scanning his gauges, Hemingway simultaneously released his brakes and jammed the throttle to full power. He sank back into his seat as the plane snapped forward.

During the 1.6 seconds the Harrier engine took coming to full power, he kept his eyes on his speed dial and at 40 knots pushed the exhaust nozzles to 60 degrees. In almost the same instant, the plane came free of the ground, having traveled little more than 200 feet.

Kevin squinted through the debris and dust thrown up by the plane, feeling both fright and exhilaration as the echoing howl of the Harrier brought pain to his ears. The slingshot takeoff was almost comparable to being catapulted off the deck of a carrier and explained why the Marines called their plane the *jump-jet*.

The White House

The red and blue clusters of flashing dots had disappeared mysteriously off the Middle East wall grid, causing irate generals and harassed communication technicians in the War Room. The technicians were also unable to make contact with the Puller or AWACs planes over the Persian Gulf.

When the VCR-110 announced, "Standby, Connie," indicating an incoming from the carrier, the President and generals hastily gathered before the wall radio.

"Admiral Johnston reporting. We have received word from the flight commander of our F-18s that they've used their exhausts to cloud up the cockpit canopies of the Ilyushins. The Russian transports are now flying blind."

The JCS Chairman moved nearer to the transmitter and spoke into its wall mike. "Have they reversed course?"

"We're not sure," came the reply. "Following this contact with the F-18s, further communications are being jammed out of the Persian Gulf. We've sent the Puller the same message I've just given you, but they've failed to acknowledge it."

"Thank you, Admiral," said Steel. "When you can, pass my congratulations to your flight commander." When he turned around, the somber expression on the face of the JCS Chairman didn't match those of the civilians in the War Room.

"Well," grinned the President, "if the Russians can't see, they can't land. They'll have to turn around."

"Not necessarily, sir," countered General Huering. He watched the grin fade and continued. "Most certainly, the soldiers in those transports are outfitted with parachutes. And the planes *could* still land if the MiG pilots talked them down. We do that ourselves in emergencies."

President Steiner nodded thoughtfully. "We'll prepare for either contingency. How do we stop them if they use parachutes?"

When the JCS Chairman hesitated, Huering volunteered, "Sir, it's possible to stop the Russians cold, regardless of how they come into Dhahran."

"Explain yourself ," said the President when the Marine general paused himself, long enough to glance at Steel who did not discourage him.

"It would involve the use of weapons which the United States disavowed back in the early eighties." Huering paused to get the President's reaction.

"Stop beating around the bush!" snapped Allan Steiner.

"In addition to standard-issue rifles," continued Huering, "our Force Recon units have recently acquired light-weight lasers. For security purposes, they're code-named CCWs, or crowd-control weapons. They have the capability of crippling nearby combat vehicles, including low-flying aircraft, or inflicting injuries of a debilitating nature on enemy soldiers.''

"What do you mean by *debilitating*.''

"One of our laser weapons is called a PBL, sir. At low intensity, it projects a hot particle beam that can cause sufficient burns to incapacitate an enemy soldier. Higher intensities can melt internal controls of a nearby aircraft, or even sever a wing.''

"What other types of laser weapons do we have?''

"Just one, sir,'' replied Huering. "The XRL— or X-ray laser. It's radar-guided and designed to counter missiles by causing violent vibrations of its target. It can also be applied to ground targets.''

Clayton Walters broke in. "May I raise a point, Mr. President? We're discussing the initiation of hostile actions against the Soviet Union, which, in the case of an in-flight aircraft, could undoubtedly result in heavy casualties. Are there other solutions we should be considering—solutions that won't give the Kremlin cause to retaliate in kind . . . or worse?''

The secretary of state sensed hostility in the War Room, or at least impatience on the faces of those around him. "I'm only reiterating, Mr. President, the words of caution you spoke to the Saudi king.''

President Steiner frowned. There was too little time to discuss further alternatives and he knew Derevenko wouldn't be interested in listening to them. Wiping his face with his hands in a hopeless gesture, the President looked up at his generals.

"I don't intend to give the Russians an excuse to escalate this affair any further than necessary. General Steel, order the Marines at Dhahran to

utilize these laser weapons to discourage the landing of transports, *without* shooting the planes
down.''

General Huering interjected: ''Mr. President,
this discussion may be academic . . . if we can't
communicate with the Puller.''

The President looked to Steel. ''I thought only
outgoing communication from the Gulf was down?''

''That's confirmed, sir. Both the AWACs and
our satellites are being jammed in that sector. We
don't know if they can receive our messages.''

''Send my order to use lasers, then. If they don't
receive it, let's hope they follow the guidelines
we've already given them for their Harriers.''

''Sir,'' began General Steel, ''what if the Soviet
troops get on the ground and—''

The President interrupted. ''If they get on the
ground, we'll use the laser weapons to *disable only.*''
To no one in particular, he added: ''I'd rather
share the Saudi oil fields with the Russians than
start a war over them.''

While the face of the JCS Chairman remained
stoic, the other military men turned aside to con-
ceal their expressions of disgust. General Steel
thought to ask the President if he was certain the
Russians would *share* the oil, but kept his counsel.

Over Western Saudi Arabia

Trying to warm her toes within the too-short blanket, Irene cuddled closer to Hamud's back as the early sun sent slivers of silver into the lingering shadows of the Lear Jet cabin. She watched the play of light with half-open eyes.

The first week of vacation in Cannes had become tedious, spending days with her sister on the gusty beach where windswept sand stung the skin of sunbathers . . . and nights in the discotheques dancing with men too short for her five-foot-eleven frame. Running into Hamud at a casino had been a stroke of luck. They'd met formally several months earlier at an embassy reception in Riyadh. Away from his native country, Hamud was the complete opposite of the quiet, dignified image he exuded in Riyadh. In the course of Irene's second week of vacation, the young man and woman had acquired an intimacy that would never have been possible in Saudi Arabia.

Much of their affinity came from a shared aimlessness, not an uncommon trait of the many youths (and those not so young) who flocked to the Riviera in search of sybaritic pleasures.

Both Hamud and Irene led lives without challenge after many years spent gathering extensive and expensive educations. Now the search for known pleasures to fill their days seemed far more natural than a search for unknown goals. And in fulfilling their mutual gratifications, they temporarily dissipated the shared guilt of their wasted lives.

When Hamud had offered to return Irene to Riyadh in his private jet, she wasn't surprised to learn it would be just the two of them, though she did become mildly concerned when Hamud directed her to occupy the copilot seat and monitor a considerable number of gauges for him during the takeoff of the two-pilot aircraft.

Unable to fall back asleep, Irene eased away from Hamud, carefully replacing the blanket against his back. Catching a glimpse of crimson through a window, she paused at the circular view. A deep red on the curved eastern rim of the earth gradually gave way to an intense orange-yellow glow that began to fill the interior of the cabin. Mesmerized, Irene jumped at the hand that cupped the nape of her neck.

"Sorry," apologized Hamud, gently caressing where he touched. "Have you never witnessed the rising sun at 25,000 feet?"

"Not until now," she replied softly, still gazing at the blossoming sunrise.

"Only a desert dawn in the Rub Al Khali is more beautiful."

Irene leaned back slightly and half-turned her head to nuzzle against Hamud. She rolled her cheek along his.

"Someday, I will show it to you," he said softly.

Irene matched her lips to his. "I would like that." She pointed to a door at the rear of the small cabin and discreetly inquired, "Is that what I think it is?"

He nodded with a smile. "There is a shower . . . but no tub, so I shall *not* accompany you." He winked. Recalling the games in the massive tub of his condo in Cannes, she grabbed for the hook of his nose and missed. Laughing as he twisted away, Hamud checked his watch. "We should arrive at Riyadh within the hour."

Emerging from the bathroom in a conservative green dress and heels, Irene joined Hamud in the cockpit. He motioned her into the copilot's seat without speaking. Letting the plane slowly descend to afford Irene a better view of the deep-shadowed mountainous desert below, Hamud leveled off and wove through occasional opalescent wisps of clouds.

Flipping the switch to his radio, Hamud broke the long silence. "Riyadh Control, this is flight XK9. Request permission to land in approximately 15 minutes. Over."

The response was immediate. "Flight XK9, this is Riyadh Control. Permission denied. Suggest alternate landing at Al Hafuf. Over."

"Riyadh Control. Flight XK9 has insufficient fuel to reach Al Hafuf," Hamud lied.

"I'm sorry, Flight XK9," said a new, British-accented voice. "We cannot clear you to land here."

"Why not?" demanded Hamud.

"We're not at liberty to explain," responded the Briton.

Hamud clicked off his radio and jovially told Irene, "We shall have to find out for ourselves why they do not wish us to land."

From a mile up, the massive arches bounding each of the ultra-modern passenger terminals of King Khalid International Airport gave the appearance of a Bedouin tent billowing in the wind. Between two of the arches at one end of the structure sat a plump mosque with its rounded dome. The 3.4-billion-dollar airport was the second largest in the world, surpassed only by a newer one in western Saudi Arabia. Its size was half-again as large as the combined runways of LAX, Kennedy, LaGuardia, and O'Hare in the United States. It had been built to the precise specifications of King Khalid to the dismay of its French architects and considerable profit of its British contractors.

Banking to the south, Hamud turned on the radio again and this time spoke in a deeper tone. "Riyadh Control. Is runway 14 clear?"

"Yes," responded the British accent, "but—"

"I have an emergency," interrupted Hamud in his new voice. "I'm coming in from the west on runway 14." He flipped off the radio before the controller could react.

As the sleek, two-engine Lear Jet screamed nearer the high-wire fence surrounding the airport's western runways, a Saudi army sergeant tracked its approach with a shoulder mounted Stinger missile, rushing through the last of the 18 steps required to activate his weapon. His orders were to fire on any aircraft attempting to land at the airport. When the plane passed directly to his front, the sergeant sighted and pulled the trigger mechanism.

Getting no response, he squeezed harder. Still nothing.

Taking the mounted missile off his shoulder, the sergeant studied its controls. A furious Saudi officer ran up and also checked the controls.

Touching the red switch in front of the trigger mechanism with his swagger stick, the lieutenant shouted, "Imbecile! You have the brains of *a flea in a goat's ass!*"

The sergeant had remembered each of the first 17 steps to release the Stinger, but had omitted the last. The safety switch still engaged the trigger, and he humbly absorbed the officer's abuse. By the time the lieutenant had exhausted his deprecations, Hamud was braking the aircraft beside his car.

"Did you see the tanks and soldiers to our left just before we landed?" asked Irene.

Hamud nodded. "There were national guardsmen as well. They must be waiting for an important visitor," he explained as he flipped switches to cut the engine.

When Hamud jerked open the cabin's door, a military jeep slid to a halt before his plane. Using a hand to caution Irene away from the door, Hamud pressed a button to lower the plane's folding ladder. He stepped out onto the first step, half-closing the door behind him. The jeep contained three armed soldiers and an officer.

"*You are under arrest!*" blurted the officer excitedly, standing in his vehicle.

Hamud snorted. "And you are a fool," calmly stated the Saudi prince as he pointed to his white convertible. "That is my car."

The men in the jeep gaped at the car. To the left and below the silver *Corniche* signature on the lid of the trunk was a gold-rimmed, green license plate identifying the owner as a member of the royal family.

Hopping out of his vehicle, the officer smartly clicked his heels before saluting. "Praise to Allah . . . a thousand pardons. We did not know who you were. Our orders are to kill any foreigners landing at the airport."

"Praise to Allah, I am no foreigner," smiled Hamud, adding, "You may go."

After another salute, the officer jumped into the jeep, and Hamud stepped back inside his plane. Irene spoke in a frightened voice.

"*Why* do they have orders to kill foreigners?"

"I didn't ask. For your sake, I wanted them to leave as soon as possible." Hamud completed dressing by placing a white thobe trimmed in gold over his western-style suit. Before snapping his suitcase shut, he removed an elaborately decorated khanjar and tucked the curved dagger and sheath in his belt.

Though Irene knew the crescent-shaped blade of the khanjar made it an ill-suited weapon, she asked with new alarm, "Do you expect trouble?"

"No," replied Hamud, patting the jewel-encrusted sheath. "This is only symbolic."

She squinted. "Of what?"

"My virility." He gave his raffish smile and let fingers run along the uplifted curve of the khanjar.

"You're kidding?" she scoffed at the sexual metaphor.

"It's an old belief in my country," Hamud explained in complete seriousness. "Come, let us go now."

After throwing their luggage in the trunk of the

convertible, they headed for the exit of the private aircraft section. At the gate, Hamud waved the Pakistani guard to his car window and asked, "Why are the army and national guard on the runways?"

"You have not heard?"

"No, I just arrived."

The sentry's eyes opened wide. "There is to be an invasion. Only a short while ago, many bombs were dropped."

"Open the gate," ordered Hamud, concluding the conversation. Instead of taking the highway toward Riyadh, he turned into the lane leading to the passenger terminals. It was clogged with both military and civilian vehicles. In the slowed traffic, Hamud lowered the top of the convertible.

"Why are we going this way?" asked Irene.

Hamud gave her a broad grin. "I want to see the *invasion*."

"I'd like to get into Riyadh," said Irene anxiously.

"*After* the invasion," he joked. Their car moved sluggishly past parking lots filled with military vehicles. Irene was amazed that none of the civilian vehicles appeared to be leaving. They outnumbered the military vehicles as they neared the terminals.

"It looks like an invasion of sightseers," she commented derisively.

Pounding his horn now like most of the other drivers, Hamud switched lanes with abandon in an effort to get closer to the terminals. After working his way into a lane near the first terminal (normally reserved for members of the royal family and exalted guests of the kingdom), Hamud threw his gearshift into "park" before bringing the Rolls to a full stop. As the transmission ground the car to a halt, he jumped out and called, "Let's go!"

Looking back at the furious drivers blasting their horns in the now blocked lane, Irene shouted to Hamud, "You can't park here!"

Oblivious to the protesting drivers, Hamud opened the passenger door to the convertible and grabbed her hand. "We'll be just a minute," he promised and rushed her into the terminal.

The chaos inside the terminal reminded Irene of minor riots she'd seen on television. Saudi men, mostly in military uniforms, rushed to and fro. Scattered groups of officers loudly argued among themselves. Scores of Saudi civilians crowded around the floor-to-ceiling windows offering views of the runways. Irene saw no other women in the terminal.

"Upstairs," directed Hamud when he realized the downstairs windows were congested already. He pulled her by the sleeve instead of her hand as they pushed their way onto an escalator.

The mezzanine was also jammed with humanity, and a larger proportion were in military uniforms. Hamud resolutely pressed into one of the throngs around a window, still gripping Irene's sleeve. There were no planes in view, either on the runways or near the terminal loading areas. After standing several minutes in the crush of the noisy men around the window, Irene jerked Hamud's arm and whispered, "If you won't take me into Riyadh, I'll—"

He shook his head. "I cannot hear you."

"I'm going to call for a car!" she shouted over the din.

Hamud released her and watched for a moment as Irene marched stiffly in high heels across the marble-floored mezzanine. She ignored the leers and taunts of some of the Saudi men, a few of whom deliberately jostled her as she passed. Knowing Saudi men often treated unescorted women in this manner, she felt no particular danger.

When Irene found a pillar containing telephones, she rapidly punched out the number of the American embassy. Getting no ring, she pressed the receiver to her ear. She shook her head and decided she'd misdialed. Irene started to dial again and gasped as a soldier locked her arms in a vise-like grip.

Twisting to scream at her assailant, Irene lost her voice. The dusky faces of two heavily armed soldiers glowered at her, and their red-and-white checkered gutras told her protest was useless. The two national guardsmen dragged her away from the telephones, in the opposite direction from which she'd come. She shouted over her shoulder for Hamud, causing one of the guardsmen to jerk her arm violently and growl, "Quiet, woman!"

Thinking Hamud either could not hear her shouts or chose to ignore them, Irene decided to remain silent. She was pulled into a uniformed group gathered around another window and Irene relaxed somewhat at the sight of the highly decorated chests of the uniforms, thinking the men must be senior officers. Her guards spoke to one of the officers, who in turn addressed a tall Saudi wearing a gold-trimmed thobe.

Irene immediately recognized Crown Prince Saleem and blurted out, "Your Highness, I'm accompanied by—"

"I have not spoken to you," Saleem interrupted in English. He glared at her a moment before flicking his wrist. "Take her to the trucks!"

"*I* will take her," countered a hard voice to the rear of Irene, who closed her eyes in relief at the sound of Hamud's words. Saleem bellowed, "*Who speaks so.*"

"A brother, Your Highness." A path instantly parted between the two equally obstinate royal princes. Hamud, fully as tall as his older half-brother, smiled as he came forward to the side of Irene. Recognizing the youngest of his 44 brothers, Saleem smirked as he spoke.

"And what would you want with such a foreigner?"

"Praise to Allah, I do not want her," Hamud said with scorn, "but she is my guest."

"You are not in your home, my brother," Saleem reminded Hamud. "Here she is *my guest.*"

When Hamud did not challenge the Crown Prince further, Saleem again ordered his guards to remove Irene and turned back to the window. Placing a hand in front of the guards, Hamud signified they should wait a moment. He pushed his way up behind his half-brother and whispered into Saleem's ear.

The Crown Prince wearily came around. Showing great contempt on his face, he waved his hand and hissed, "I do not want her."

Hamud grabbed Irene's arm and roughly pulled her away from Saleem's group.

"You're *hurting* me," Irene protested. He lightened his grip, but did not slow their pace until they were on the escalator back to the ground floor. Coming off the escalator, he asked, "Do you have tennis shoes in your baggage?"

Irene nodded, and he pulled her outside to his car. When they returned inside the terminal, Irene had exchanged tennis shoes for the heels and wore Hamud's thobe (turned inside-out) over her dress. Hamud had fashioned an *abaya* about her head with a blue shirt and it shielded all but her eyes from the staring men. This time they remained on the lower level, well away from the escalators.

Dhahran Airbase

As his Harrier orbited the Control Tower at Dhahran, Hemingway keyed his mike. "Hammer, this is Gorilla 101. Come in."

"Hammer, here," responded Lt. Colonel Banks promptly.

"What's your progress?"

"Both objectives secured."

"Any problems?"

"None. Right after we went into the tower, the Saudi area commander showed up . . . a General Lakar. He's been cooperative, so I've positioned his men in the southern sector of the base. We've also borrowed jeeps and armored vehicles from them."

"Excellent," said Hemingway. "Where are their F-15s?"

"They tangled with the Russians, and according to Lakar only two F-15s survived."

"Saudis do any damage?"

"None claimed."

Poor bastards, mused Hemingway, *all they know how to do is point and pray.* And he wondered how his Harrier squadron would fare against the Fulcrums. "How many men do you still have undeployed?"

"Half."

102

"Any ideas on how to keep the Commies out of here?"

"PBLs," suggested Banks. "Give 'em a warm welcome."

Hemingway considered the last message from the Puller. It had stressed not to initiate any form of deadly fire on the Soviets . . . yet he was supposed to discourage their landing.

"That might work too well," allowed Hemingway. "If someone hit one of their fuel-lines, it'd look like a missile hit and all hell'd break loose."

"That reminds me," Banks said. "We talked Lakar into giving us control of all their Stinger and Hawk missiles."

"How'd you do that?"

"I explained to him the Commies can track them back to their sources and retaliate instantly . . . then I told him we'd assume the risk for them."

"Good work, Hammer," stated Hemingway. "I'd suggest you use your XRLs instead of the PBLs. That way, the Commies won't even know what's hitting—"

"Gorilla 101, this is 103," interrupted one of the other Harrier pilots. "Want another idea?"

"What's on your mind, 103?"

"Why not litter some of this A-Rab oil on the runways? That way the Commies'll have a helluva time coming in. If the first ones smash up, it oughta discourage the rest of 'em."

"I like it," said Banks instantly.

"So do I," agreed Hemingway. "My Stallions could haul drums from the fuel dump and spread oil on the runways. Your men could commandeer all the aviation refuelers on the base and do the same.''

"Consider it done," concluded Banks.

"Hammer, have you heard from Pounder in the last five minutes?" asked Hemingway. Pounder was the radio designation for their commander, Colonel Moore, who was still on the Puller.

"Negative."

"I can't raise him on the radio," revealed Hemingway, "so I'm going back to Truckstop to check it out."

"Before you go," said Banks, "do you mind if I park a dozen of your Stallions around the Control Tower . . . to make our presence known?"

"Good idea, Hammer. Just don't leave any men in them." Hemingway checked his watch. "Our friends are due in 55 minutes. I'll check back with you after seeing Pounder."

The White House

After the President's brief summary for the seated three-member congressional delegation, Speaker of the House Edward Snell asked, "Can the Russians still land?"

President Steiner fiddled with his ear. After three months in office, he was still uncomfortable when forced to formulate replies to questions he had no idea how to answer. It wasn't the slight misinformation he occasionally provided that bothered him. What stung his conscience was when he found himself attempting to portray an overly optimistic view which he knew to be unrealistic.

"It's unlikely"—Allan Steiner frowned at himself—"for reasons we've already outlined."

Snell switched his attention to the JCS Chairman. "General, if the Russians *do* manage to land at Dhahran, what do we do then?"

"We haven't had time to develop a detailed plan other than to instruct our field commanders to use measures which minimize potential casualties."

Hoolihan whispered into the ear of the President, who nodded and added, "We also called Derevenko to tell him our Marines have already invaded Saudi Arabia." Becoming increasingly conscious of his overuse of 'we' as if he sought a shared responsibility for his actions, the President made a mental note to avoid this posturing.

Senator Winslow, Senate minority leader and a member of the President's party, asked, "What was Derevenko's reaction?"

"He said the Afghan flight was a training mission . . . that we should not be concerned about it." The President added, "This was before the AWACs notified us of the flight coming from South Yemen."

"Pardon me for saying so, Mr. President," commented Snell, "but this is a goddamn mess."

President Steiner started to openly agree when the Senate majority leader, Joe Farrell, spoke up in a sour tone. "I find this all quite hard to believe, Mr. President. You were elected on a peace platform . . . and now you're authorizing actions which could lead to global war."

"On the contrary," the President promptly rejoined, "the actions I've authorized are geared to prevent that possibility."

"How can you say that," pressed Farrell, "considering what the F-18s have done already to the Soviet planes? For God's sake, do you realize *the risks* you're taking?"

Farrell went on. "We're now in a position to start a major conflict over a semi-friendly Arab country that supplies us with less than five percent of our oil imports. If Asad had wanted to avoid a foreign takeover, he should have requested our military presence long before this."

Allan Steiner inwardly smiled, thinking *I had enough trouble getting the perfidious fool to accept our assistance now.*

Snell leaned forward, pointing his finger at the Middle East wall grid. "How can you be certain the destination of the Soviet flights are, in fact, Saudi Arabia? It could be Iraq . . . or even Kuwait. Have we contacted people in those countries to determine their involvement? With the Iranians on the warpath, either of those countries might have invited the Russians into the Persian Gulf area."

Though of the same party as the President, Snell had developed his speakership in a curmudgeon style. He considered himself above party lines and displayed a smug superiority to those who were mere members of partisan parties.

"Mr. Speaker," the President coyly remarked, "I find your suggestion highly improbable. If Derevenko had no designs on the Saudi oil fields, it would be in his interests to tell us openly . . . and thereby avoid the possibility of confrontation with us. He would certainly have stated his planes were simply utilizing Saudi airspace to reach Iraq or Kuwait, if that were the case."

President Steiner switched to Farrell. "As for the F-18s, we gave them explicit orders not to fire unless fired upon."

Farrell threw up his hands. "What difference does it make *who* fires first?" he contended. "Either way, it could expand into World War III! We don't need that . . . not over Saudi Arabia, or any other *fickle-minded Arab country.*"

The President stood and spoke with a trace of irritability. "Gentlemen, I've called you down here to inform you of the current situation in the Persian Gulf. If you have positive suggestions how this crisis can be resolved, please offer them." He paused to look each politician in the eye. "I'm acting in what I believe to be the best interests of the United States. So far, we *are not* in a global conflict . . . or even a limited conflict with the Soviets."

"Mr. President," began the Speaker, "may I remind you of the War Powers Act of 1973? The President is required to report to Congress within 48 hours of ordering American troops into hostile situations."

"I'm quite aware of my responsibilities, Mr. Speaker," replied the President evenly. Wishing to keep the politicians away from the media, he added, "In order to keep you informed of the latest developments, may I suggest you remain in the White House?"

Receiving no objections, the President addressed his assistant. "Jim, escort these gentlemen to the Oval Office." As they filed out of the War Room, Farrell muttered to his small group, "This is a fine time to have *a rookie* in the White House!"

A uniformed aide approached President Steiner. "Sir, the director of the CIA is on line 8. He says it's urgent."

The President reluctantly picked up the phone. "What is it, Mr. Rolle?"

"We've just received a message from Riyadh that I wanted to relay to you personally."

"What is it?"

"The Saudi Land and Air Forces *will* cooperate with us," revealed Rolle matter-of-factly.

"How do you know that?" asked the President. "Only thirty minutes ago, the king and his brothers said they wouldn't."

Rolle's voice was friendly. "Sir, the Saudis seldom say what they mean, even among themselves.''

Thinking *I've heard that before,* Allan Steiner asked, ''What's your source?''

The CIA director paused significantly. ''I'd rather not say over the phone, sir. Perhaps, I should come over.''

Having intentionally kept Rolle—a holdover of the previous administration—out of the War Room, President Steiner debated his reply. He had found approval of the earlier CIA participation in Kuwait distasteful, even though the placement of the flu-compound in the Kuwait water supply had been disguised as an act of the Iraqi army. He was anxious to minimize Rolle's subsequent role in the crisis. And personally, the self-confident, almost contemptuous manner of the man aggravated him.

Still awaiting the President's reply, Rolle asked, ''May I pose a question, sir?''

''Go ahead.''

Fully aware of the presidential coolness, Rolle spoke cautiously. ''Why hasn't Admiral Johnston ordered our F-18s to proceed to Dhahran after refueling in Oman?''

In the silence that followed, the CIA director considered how he might rephrase his words.

President Steiner responded with his own question. ''How the hell do you know they're in Oman?''

''That's my job, sir.''

''Get yourself over here,'' ordered Allan Steiner, who immediately implemented Rolle's suggestion.

Dhahran Airbase

Joining up with the other Harriers, Hemingway ordered five of his aircraft to hide on the base, going under tactical control of Colonel Banks. The other two Harriers were directed to assume positions off his starboard wing.

"We're headed east," explained Hemingway, "to see why Truckstop's not talking."

At the shoreline of the Gulf, Hemingway snapped, "Move it up to 500 knots!"

A moment later, one of his wingmen exclaimed, "There's smoke coming—"

"I know," interrupted Hemingway. He'd already seen the black column of smoke rising from the water north of the island of Bahrain. At three miles, the pilots recognized the Puller—fire and smoke curling up its port side. A destroyer escort was beside the crippled ship.

"Circle at 3K," ordered Hemingway. "I'm going in."

After setting his Harrier down roughly, Hemingway jumped to the deck and raised a fist with his thumb out at a purple-shirt (fueler). He jerked the fist to his mouth like a Coke bottle, signaling he wanted fuel, and then sprinted to Flight Deck Control. Finding it deserted, he ran back onto the flight deck and grabbed the nearest seaman.

"What happened here?" Hemingway demanded.

"Two hits!" blurted the seaman, wide-eyed and near panic. "We took two hits from a gunboat."

Hemingway raced up the outside ladders to the bridge and found the Puller's skipper barking orders to several men. Seeing the Harrier commander, the skipper stared at him a moment. "Why're you back?"

Without answering, Hemingway asked his own question. "How'd you get it?"

"A Saudi gunboat, patrolling 200 yards to port, dropped two torpedoes on us." The ship's commander winced. "Wasn't a damn thing we could do."

"Where's Colonel Moore?" inquired Hemingway.

The skipper winced again. "Dead. His helo took a missile from the gunboat right after he lifted off. The torpedoes followed. They must have been waiting for him."

"Where's the gunboat?"

"In a couple thousand pieces," explained the shipper. "The destroyer blew it out of the water."

Hemingway jerked his head toward Bahrain. "Can you make the beach over there?"

Gawking at the flames licking over the edge of his flight deck, the skipper shook his head. "It may not be worth trying . . . if we can't get those fires under control. They'll reach our forward magazines in another twenty minutes."

"You'd better get your men onto the destroyer," suggested Hemingway.

The skipper nodded. "You'd do well to get off quick, too."

"Good luck!" called Hemingway, stepping off the bridge. Rejoining the two other Harriers, he headed back toward Dhahran. Before they reached the coast, one of his wingman broke radio silence.

"Gorilla 101, this is 103. Six bogeys coming up fast at seven o'clock."

"103 and 105, this is 101. Take a 1500-foot step-up, reduce speed to 325 knots, and standby to viff."

Three MiGs came up tight on Hemingway's aircraft—one on each wingtip at 20 yards and the third behind and below him. Each of the other Harriers picked up a similar trio. Hemingway glanced to his port side and, for the first time in his life, saw a Fulcrum up close. The AV-8B was dwarfed by the MiG-29, which was a full third larger. Each of the MiG's twin engines had the same thrust as the Harrier's single power plant, giving the Soviet pilot a top speed more than double his counterpart. In addition, the Fulcrum had been designed as an air superiority fighter. Hemingway was not particularly concerned.

He gradually maneuvered nearer the port Fulcrum, placing the tip of his wing within five yards of the Russian's wingtip. Getting the Soviet's attention, the American raised his right hand and displayed three fingers. As the Fulcrum pilot stared back, Hemingway successively flashed one finger, four fingers, and two fingers . . . then pointed to his ear.

The Russian nodded.

Setting his UHF radio at 314.2 and keying his mike, the American pilot asked, "Do you read me?"

Hemingway heard guttural tones of several Russian voices over the signaled frequency. A voice asked him in crude English, "Who are you?"

"I'm with the American military forces at Dhahran air base," said Hemingway. "I want to speak to your flight commander."

More jabbering filled his headset.

The English-speaking pilot replied, "Commander not speak your language."

"Tell him," Hemingway stated succinctly, "United States Marines . . . occupy . . . Dhahran air base."

The MiG pilot came right back. "My commander say Marines leave Dhahran *at once!*"

The eastern shoreline of Saudi Arabia passed below. In a matter of a few minutes, they'd be over the air base. Hemingway's tone became severe. "I repeat. United States Marines hold Dhahran. You *cannot* land there. It will be—"

"How you say it, American?" interrupted the Soviet pilot. "Piss off!"

Hitting the UHF button, Hemingway growled, "Slide!"

Yanking their exhaust nozzles into breaking positions, the American pilots strained forward in their straps as their engines made a furious racket. The instant deceleration matched an arrested landing on a carrier deck as each of the Harriers squatted nearly motionless in midair. In less than three seconds, the hunted became the hunters—the Americans had neatly slid into deadly positions behind the MiGs.

A half-mile directly to his front, Hemingway now observed the tight formation of Fulcrums which moments before had been his escorts. "Goddamn," he muttered forlornly at the golden and forbidden opportunity. Within a few more seconds, he knew his Harriers could effortlessly slip Sidewinders up the exhausts of the MiGs.

The Fulcrums, realizing they'd been polewhacked, briskly broke into erratic turns and dives to reduce the American advantage. Hemingway kept his wingmen in their stepups as they came over Dhahran.

Due to his warning, Hemingway correctly surmised the Soviet commander would first do a flyby at the air base to assess the American presence. When Hemingway observed a second group of MiGs coming over the base, he keyed his mike.

"Hammer, this is Gorilla 101. Hold your fire. We are escorting MiGs over your positions." Hemingway's message was meaningless, and Banks responded accordingly.

"This is Hammer, Gorilla 101. Roger your last."

These words were also received and interpreted for the perplexed Colonel Tupolov. As he flew over Dhahran at 2500 feet, he clearly observed the circle of Sea Stallions gathered around the Control Tower. Tupolov also detected small numbers of Marines atop the buildings overlooking the runways. On a second flyby at lower altitude, Tupolov was reassured to find the Americans on the rooftops were not armed with missiles. Noting a wetness on the runways at the lower height, he wondered why a heavy morning dew had not been included in the briefings back in Kandahar.

American Embassy—Riyadh

"Are all personnel on this floor?" asked Ambassador Clark.

"Yes, sir," replied Fricke in a hushed tone. "We're ready to roll."

"Let's talk to Asad now." Clark walked across the communications room to where the Saudi king sat. Picking up a memo pad, Fricke followed and casually stationed himself near the Royal Guard officer leaning against the wall behind Asad.

"Your Majesty," began Clark, "we have been ordered by President Steiner to evacuate the embassy."

Asad froze in his chair.

Clark tried to smile. "We'd like you to go with us, Your Majesty."

The Royal guard officer came off the wall, his hand going to his holster. As the astounded king groped for a reply, Clark encouragingly added, "It's for your own protection, Your Majesty."

Drawing his gun, the Saudi officer pointed it once more at Clark. *"I* will protect my king!" he declared.

Watching the eyes of the officer, Fricke in a deliberately slow motion flipped his memo pad toward the ceiling. In the split second the officer glanced up, Fricke gripped the muzzle of the gun and forced it down.

When the officer moved his other hand to the pistol, Fricke buried the edge of his free hand in the soft plexus of the Saudi's neck. Doubling over, the bug-eyed Saudi released his gun and grasped his neck.

Fricke calmly emptied the gun's cylinder of its bullets and, placing the ammunition in his pocket, offered it back to its owner. Shaking his head in mock disapproval, Fricke said, "It's bad manners to point a gun at someone."

As the Saudi officer made no attempt to retrieve his pistol, Fricke reached over and jammed it back in its holster. The still-baffled king looked to Ambassador Clark, who smiled apologetically.

"Your Majesty, should the invasions succeed, you can take sanctuary with the Americans. We'll hide you until it is safe to leave the country."

"I do not wish to leave," Asad weakly protested.

Clark continued. "President Steiner asked me to remind you of the fate the Afghan leader met after the Soviets invaded his country in 1979. You must remember how Hafizullah Amin was hunted down like a dog and shot within 72 hours . . . and *he* was a Marxist."

"But my people"—Asad glanced at his Royal Guard officer—"will protect me."

"If that is true," Clark argued, "why are the many palaces of the Saud family guarded by Pakistani troops instead of *your people?*"

The frightened king was too disconcerted to reply.

Clark nodded to Fricke, who summoned a Marine sergeant to his side. "Sergeant Hoctor, notify everyone we leave in one minute. And assign two men to escort the Royal Guard officer. He's coming with us, too."

The sergeant returned to the door of the communications room in less than a minute and gave a thumbs-up signal.

"Hit the seals!" snapped Fricke.

Hoctor began breaking the plastic seals protecting a bank of locks by the door. As he inserted a key into each lock, tear gas hissed from fire extinguisher nozzles in the ceilings of the floors below.

"Let's go!" said Fricke, leading the way up a narrow staircase. Emerging on the roof, the Americans and their reluctant guests climbed into the waiting helicopter, its blades already churning. After conferring with Clark, Fricke informed the pilot to take them first to the nearby Lockheed compound. As they lifted off, the ambassador's eyes met those of Asad. Clark looked away hastily, wishing to avoid the accusing eyes of the Saudi king.

When they arrived over the Lockheed compound, a small international conclave of the firm's employees, Fricke shouted to the ambassador, "There's not much activity down there."

The streets were deserted within the walled compound of some three dozen western-style homes. After the pilot landed at its center, Sergeant Hoctor placed four Marines in defensive positions around the helicopter before running to the door of the nearest house. When no one responded to his knocking, he cautiously entered the home.

When the Marine sergeant came out, he appeared pale and shaken. Hoctor stepped off the sidewalk by the front door and leaned against the wall of the home to retch.

"Dammit!" exclaimed Fricke, jumping from the helicopter and sprinting toward the house.

Hoctor held up his hand to halt Fricke. "Major, you *don't* want to go in there."

Fricke pointed to an adjacent house. "Check that home, too." Entering the first house, Fricke emerged a few moments later with a stony face and walked stiffly to the helicopter.

Sergeant Hoctor shouted, "It's the same over here, sir."

Fricke continued toward the helicopter. At its open hatch, he leaned in and stared hard at Asad. "Mr. Ambassador, I think you and our *Saudi friends* should come take a look."

Clark stood and, with a motion of his arm, invited the king and his officer to precede him. Fricke waved the two Marine guards away from the Saudi officer and then followed behind the three men as they approached the house. At the open door, Asad could see enough and halted.

"I do not wish to enter," the king announced.

The ambassador stood to Asad's right, and the Saudi officer stood on his left. Fricke broke the stalemate. He violently shoved the officer from behind, and the Saudi staggered through the front door, struggling to keep his balance. Placing his hands on the backs of both Clark and Asad, Fricke applied minimal pressure as he said, "It gets worse."

The king meekly followed his Royal Guard officer inside. Both Saudis shuddered at the carnage, as Clark and Fricke crowded in behind.

Except for what clothes remained on them, mutilations made it difficult to distinguish the sex or ages of the bodies which hung on the furniture and strewed the floor. A small dog had been gutted, it entrails spilling from its twisted body.

"MY GOD," Clark gulped to the Saudi king. "Are *these* the 'infidels' your brother spoke of this morning in my office?"

Asad stared at the far wall of the living room, unable to view the bloodbath any longer.

Stepping forward, Fricke knelt down and picked up the limp body of a child—a boy of two or three. Cradling the body in his arms, Fricke faced the Saudi king and spoke hoarsely. *"Take this child!"*

Asad neither moved nor acknowledged the American's words.

With a fury burning in his eyes, Fricke came nearer and repeated his words in a low, clipped growl.

As the king gradually lifted his arms to accept the child, Fricke gently pushed the bloody body to Asad's chest. "If you drop this child," Fricke cautioned, "so help me, I'll—"

"It's time we left, Major," Clark interjected. As they walked from the home, Fricke instructed Sergeant Hoctor to have the Marines check for survivors in the rest of the compound. A few minutes later, Hoctor reported a body count of 117. One of his Marines had returned with a slight, middle-aged Oriental man. Fricke asked his Marine escort, "Where'd you find *him*?"

"He was kneeling outside one of the houses, sir. Praying or something."

Fricke addressed the man. "Who are you?"

The dismal eyes of the man were swollen and red. "My name Lee Chun. I am Korean."

What're you doing here?

Nodding in the direction of his escort, Chun said, "As I tell this one, I pray for spirits of my friends."

"Friends?" queried Fricke.

"Today my day off," the Korean said. "I come to visit friends—Jim Agnew and family."

"Were you here when this happened?"

The Korean stared sadly at his interrogator. "I think I not be talking now . . . if I be here then. When my bus come compound gate, I see many, many truck going out. Many soldier, making much noise."

"Mr. Chun," the American ambassador solemnly inquired, "what color were their head-dresses?"

The Korean paused. "I think white and red."

Clark pivoted to Asad. "The United States will hold *you personally responsible* for the people murdered here by your national guardsmen."

"Ambassador," Asad weakly replied, "the United States attacked my country. Your planes dropped bombs at Riyadh airport."

"Ours was a mock attack," Clark stated bitterly. "Before this day ends, your own children may suffer the same fate as the child in your arms . . . from a *real* attack!"

Asad dropped his eyes to the body in his arms.

"Mr. Chun," Clark said, "I'd like you to come with us. We're going to the ARAMCO compound for safety."

The Saudi king looked up in alarm. "We cannot

go there!'' he exclaimed. ''The Russians will be at Dhahran.''

''They may be,'' Clark replied, ''but I think they'll leave ARAMCO alone. There're too many Westerners there . . . and it's big enough to hide you.''

''Mr. Ambassador,'' said Fricke, ''do you plan to try and warn the other Western compounds here in Riyadh?''

Clark grimaced as he looked back at the house he'd entered. He shook his head. ''We'd be powerless to keep this from happening . . . or too late. Let's try to make ARAMCO.''

They re-entered the helicopter and before its rotor drowned out his voice, Clark turned to the Saudi king. ''Your Majesty, do you realize at least half the families in the Lockheed compound were French and British?''

As the helicopter passed over the outskirts of the Riyadh, its pilot sent word back to Clark that company was coming. Two F-15s with markings of the Royal Saudi Air Force closed at high speed, overshooting the helicopter by a mile. Circling back, the fighters took up positions on either side of the helicopter and indicated they wished to communicate with its pilot. Receiving no response, the nearest F-15 came closer, attempting to alter the helicopter's course. When this too proved ineffective, the F-15 backed off and fired a burst of 20mm rounds in front of the helicopter.

The American pilot called the ambassador to his cockpit. ''We're in trouble, sir. These boys mean business!''

''Can they force us to land?'' asked Clark.

"They can do worse," replied the pilot. "May I make a suggestion?"

Clark nodded.

"Let's slide the hatch open back there and hold the king where they can see him. If they recognize Asad, they won't fire on us again."

Clark asked, "Can we do that safely?"

"We'll tie a harness to him."

"Okay, let's try it," Clark said.

"Send Major Fricke up here," requested the pilot, "and I'll tell him what to do."

The scheme worked. The Saudi fighter pilots backed off as expected and escorted the embassy helicopter for the balance of its flight.

Dhahran Air Base

For those at ground level, the vapors from various jet fuels created steamy mirages on the runways of Dhahran Air Base. High above, Hemingway squinted into the morning sun in search of the main flight of Soviet planes as Colonel Tupolov issued his final instructions.

"Comrades, there are no military targets on the runways other than small barriers of barrels. We will land according to plan. A pair of Fulcrums will precede each transport of the first wave to clear its runways."

After Tupolov assigned pairs of Fulcrums to clear the four preselected runways and three more MiGs to knock out the helicopters gathered at the Control Tower, he told them, "You will coordinate your attacks immediately prior to touchdown of the first wave. We must not give the enemy time to react before the Ilyushins are on the ground."

The well-rehearsed plan Tupolov intended to execute consisted of an initial wave of four Ilyushins landing simultaneously on separate runways near each side of the Control Tower. This accomplished, the remaining transports would land in successive waves around the strategic center of the air base.

What seemed like specks on the canopy of Hem-

123

ingway's Harrier soon became a swarm of enemy
aircraft . . . approaching at 3500 feet. For an instant, he thought of the long-bodied brunette reaching up for him a scant two hours earlier. As his
mind switched back to the approaching danger, he
regretted he had no children by her . . . or any
other woman.

The first four Ilyushins, each with an escorting
MiG, lumbered over the airfield from the east at a
height of 500 feet. A mile from the Control Tower,
the transports were at 300 feet when they separated
for their respective runways.

The Fulcrums assigned to destroy the barriers
and helicopters came screaming in ahead of the Ilyushins. Their 20mm cannon fire scattered the
stacks of barrels like bowling pins, and tracers
kicked up pockets of flames where they came in
contact with the soaked runways. Where other
tracers found the fuel tanks of the Sea Stallions,
brilliant fireballs erupted.

The smile on Colonel Tupolov's face at these initial explosions turned to bewilderment—then
alarm—as sheets of flames raced along the runways, enveloping his transports just as they neared
touchdown.

"Pull up!" shrieked Tupolov, echoing the instructions the Ilyushin pilots were already receiving
from their escorting MiGs.

Orange flames licked at the undercarriages of the
four planes as their engines struggled against the
heat and smoke created by the oxygen-sucking in-
ferno. As the flames flashed ahead of the transports,
turning the entire airfield into a sea of fire, the

crackling roar of the blaze obliterated the howl of the straining Ilyushins.

Tips of flames scorched the bellies of the transports, and the paratroopers within tore at their seatbelts to get off their super-heated metal benches. Standing in the pitching transports provided only temporary relief, as the floor grating soon seared their feet as well.

The four Ilyushins gained little altitude until reaching the perimeter of the blazing airfield, at which point the men inside two of the planes opened doors to dissipate the heat within. This had little immediate effect, so a few men opted to jump from the transports, triggering a stampede by the others. Most of the Russians jumped from heights less than 500 feet, well under the 700 feet required to hit the ground safely. While Colonel Tupolov watched the action below in horror, Hemingway spoke into his mike.

"Hammer, this is Gorilla 101. Commies have jumped from planes at east and west ends of air base. Suggest you send two helos of men to each location. Use your Harriers for east. I will cover the west."

"Gorilla 101, this is Hammer. Helos on the way."

Hemingway hit his UHF button. "Gorillas 103 and 105, this is 101. Fly cap for me. I'm heading to west end of field." Out of respect for any SAMs (surface-to-air missiles), Hemingway kept a half-mile distance from the western Russians until the Sea Stallions approached.

When the helicopters touched down and discharged their men, Hemingway watched the Marines cautiously come up on the ragged line of Soviet paratroopers still stretched out over a distance of 600 yards. Instead of training their weapons on the Marines, it appeared most of the Russians were struggling with their feet. Establishing contact with the American ground commander, Hemingway asked:

"What the hell's going on down there?"

"This is Hammer Three. These suckers are in pretty bad shape, sir. The rubber of their footgear has melted onto their feet. The ones who've gotten their boots off have removed half their skin as well. Most of them appear to have fractured legs or serious back injuries, too."

"Hammer Three, move the Russians into a tighter group and keep your men close to them. If the MIGs come down, you may need them for cover."

Thinking of his helos, the ground commander came back. "Sir, why don't we gather the Commies around the two Stallions?"

"Make it happen!" agreed Hemingway, turning his Harrier to the east.

At the eastern edge of the airfield, elements of the Saudi army had reached the planeload of Russian paratroopers first. By the time the Marines arrived, the Saudis were expending the last of their ammunition into the inert bodies of the Russians.

As the Americans approached, the Saudi soldiers began prancing among the grotesquely turned bodies, loudly proclaiming their "victory." A few busily looted the corpses.

Seeing no casualties among the Saudis, the

American commander commented to a Marine NCO: "Doesn't look like much of a firefight."

The NCO studied the contorted positions of the bodies. "The Commies didn't put up much resistance," he concurred. "Only a few were holding weapons when they bought it."

A nearby Marine, removing a small camera from his pack, began taking pictures of the dancing Saudis.

"Put that away, you moron!" barked a sergeant.

The American commander wheeled around and eyed the Marine with the camera. "That's all right," countermanded the officer. "Take some more . . . just keep *the Saudis* in the background. And when you're finished, give me the roll of film." To the Marine sergeant, he explained: "I want proof who did this."

At one end of the line of bodies, a looting soldier jumped up and placed an object on the tip of his rifle's bayonet. Screaming: "Allah Akbar! Allah Akbar!" he strutted among the other Saudis who quickly joined in his cry.

As this crazed procession approached the Americans, a tall Marine raised the butt of his rifle and clipped the chin of the Saudi holding the bloody object aloft on his bayonet.

The Saudi collapsed, dropping his rifle. The blonde head of a young Russian hit the ground with a thud . . . still fixed to the bayonet.

The stunned Saudis fell silent, some lowering their rifles menacingly at the Marines and muttering muffled threats. The Americans leveled their weapons, awaiting an order from their commander.

The Saudi soldiers began backing off.

"You . . . Marine!" thundered the American commander.

Everyone froze and looked to the officer, who was pointing at the tall Marine standing over the still-prone Saudi.

"You!" repeated the officer to the tall Marine. "Pick up his rifle and return it to him."

The Marine gawked at his commander.

"That's an order!" bellowed the officer.

As the Marine stooped to pick up the Saudi rifle holding the head of the Russian, the American officer called out: "Where's the camera?"

Its owner swiftly came forward.

Indicating the head, the officer told him: "Get some more pictures."

The flattened Saudi staggered to his feet and warily accepted the rifle. When it was in his hands again, another Saudi howled:

"Allah Akbar!"

As the Saudis resumed their celebration, the Marine commander shook his head and commented to his NCO: "You know, Sergeant . . . I thought I'd seen it all in Nam, but these Arabs take the cake."

"They're having more fun," the NCO drawled disgustingly, "than pigs in shit."

"When the camera's out of film," stated the officer "disarm the bastards. Kick ass, if you have to."

"With pleasure," the NCO replied. "What about the head?" The officer watched the blonde head bouncing above the Arabs a moment. "Put it back where it belongs."

Hemingway, appearing overhead, keyed his mike. "This is Gorilla 101. Give me a report."

"This is Hammer Four," replied the ground commander. "The Russians were slaughtered by the Saudis before we arrived. We've taken photos of it."

Hemingway glanced overhead for MiGs. "Check for survivors."

An NCO ordered two squads of Marines down each end of the line of fallen Russians.

"We don't want word to get out what's happened here," Hemingway cautioned. "I suggest you secure the nearest building and place the bodies inside."

"What about the Saudis, sir?"

"Keep them in the building, too. Isolate the Saudis until we decide what to do with them."

The NCO returned and reported to the ground commander, who relayed his words to Hemingway. "We have two survivors, but they've got more holes in them than a piece of Swiss cheese."

"Put them in a helo," ordered Hemingway, "and get them back to"—he paused, remembering the Puller had been hit—"Tell the helo to head southeast toward the ARAMCO compound. There's a small hospital there . . . a light yellow, four-story building."

Listening to the interpretation of Hemingway's exchange with his ground commander, Colonel Tupolov trembled as he switched his radio to its home base frequency. "Hilltop, this is Cossack."

"We read you, Cossack," came through the static. "This is Hilltop."

The Russian flight commander chose his words with great care. "Have attempted four landings without success. Airfield is burning, and Americans occupy objective.''

"How does an airfield burn, Cossack?''

"It is burning,'' Tupolov repeated. "The flames reach to 100 feet.''

"Can the Ilyushins land next to *your* burning airfield?''

Tupolov debated. "I cannot be certain. Terrain is sandy and irregular.'' Hoping to discourage the idea, he added, "The Ilyushins may be unable to take off after landing.''

"That is of no consequence, Cossack. How many Americans have you observed?''

Tupolov's answer was given hesitantly. "Eight fighter aircraft and 200 men on the ground with helicopters.''

"Don't waste our time! *Land your planes,* Cossack.''

"It would be better to use parachutes,'' suggested Tupolov.

"We must have the tanks. Follow your orders immediately!''

Tupolov blurted out: "But the Ilyushin pilots cannot see to land!''

"Then land further from the smoke, imbecile!'' came the furious reply.

"It is not the smoke,'' replied Tupolov, knowing his next words would seal his fate. "The transport pilots cannot see out their cockpits.''

The raging voice was clear over the static. *"Why? Why* can our pilots not see out their cockpits?''

"Americans scorched their canopies with the afterburners of their F-18s,'' admitted Tupolov. In the ensuing silence, he added: "I have assigned a Fulcrum to escort each transport."

The radio was still as his superiors conferred. Their orders came within the minute. "Cossack, land a transport immediately on the best terrain available near the airfield. We await your report."

The Russian flight commander dropped to 800 feet and circled the air base. The uneven ground of the perimeter contained a haphazard array of abandoned aircraft, fuel trucks, and other vehicles—disguised in varying degrees by the sand.

Tupolov rejoined his transports and maneuvered to the side of an Ilyushin, relieved its MiG escort and closed to twenty meters of the transport's port wingtip.

"Comrade," began Tupolov calmly, "I will guide you to a safe landing outside the airfield. Do exactly as I say."

Concern was evident in the Ilyushin pilot's voice. "Cossack, I require a minimum of 200 meters to land on rough terrain . . . and that is with a touchdown speed of 140 kilometers."

Both men knew the MiG-29 stalled at no less than 155 kilometers per hour and therefore could not properly escort the Ilyushin to touchdown. Tupolov made the only choice available.

"Comrade," he said, "you will land at a speed of 160 kilometers. Commence descent now, and I will control your direction."

Tupolov halted the descent at 150 meters and guided the transport to the west side of the runways where he'd seen a suitable site. Slowing their airspeed to 165 kilometers, the Russian commander felt fear for the first time this day. One hundred and fifty meters was insufficient altitude to regain control of his Fulcrum if it stalled.

"I do not like this," whined the Ilyushin pilot. "By the time you give me corrections, it may be too late to respond."

"Just do as I say. Everything is fine," assured his commander. Approaching the optimal terrain, Tupclov eased the transport down below twenty five meters.

"You are now ten meters off the ground," announced Tupolov. "Lower your speed and land."

The Ilyushin pilot hesitated in lowering his speed; and Tupolov, realizing the transport would touch down past the ideal terrain, veered away and shouted a last instruction.

"Get your nose up!"

The pilot of the Ilyushin—unable to visually correct his error—compounded it. The overcompensation brought the tail of his plane into the ground where it rebounded, causing the front of the fuselage to seesaw downward. The nose of the transport dug deep into the soft sand, plowing into the carcass of a half-buried truck.

As the tail of the aircraft lifted high in the air, a tank within ripped from its moorings and tipped the plane onto its port wing. The Ilyushin stood suspended in air a moment . . . before pancaking upside-down. A large cloud of sand enshrouded its position.

Twisting his MiG around, Tupolov winced as a knot of red flames and smoke replaced the suspended sand about the transport. He keyed his mike.

"Hilltop, this is Cossack. Landing attempted on best terrain. Aircraft destroyed."

The reply was quick. "Cossack, this is Hilltop. Abort. Repeat . . . abort. Tankers will refuel over Strait of Hormuz."

After the Soviet commander regrouped his flight and gave it a bearing to the southeast, he considered his options: A single bullet from his pistol . . . the strychnine tablet in his emergency packet . . . or . . .

He was too loyal a party member to seriously consider the third option.

ARAMCO

Following the withdrawing Ilyushin flight, Hemingway continued over the Persian Gulf to the spot where he'd left the Puller. He found the assault carrier's destroyer escort steaming near a large oil slick filled with debris. Unable to get anything but white noise in his attempts to talk with the destroyer, he turned back to Dhahran. Over the air base again, he keyed his mike.

"Hammer, this is Gorilla 101. Red Dog flight's over the Gulf now. I'm heading for ARAMCO to try and raise JCS." Hemingway dispatched his wingmen to fly cap over the air base and turned south. As he passed over the giant ARAMCO compound this time, he picked out the movie theater, radio and TV station, hospital, schools, stores, office buildings, and other facilities of the self-contained township. The 15,000 Westerners and non-Saudi Arabs within were isolated from the surrounding local population by an eight-foot wall with gates controlled by Lebanese and Yemeni guards.

The compound had been built for the American employees of the Arabia American Oil Company, commonly known as ARAMCO; and even after the Saudis assumed control of the company, the Westerners who provided management and technical

134

assistance to the country's oil industry had continued to grow in number.

The purpose of the wall was not to keep the Westerners inside as much as it was to keep the Saudis
outside, away from the "contaminated" way of life
in Little America. Bacon, a forbidden item to Mus-
lims, was readily available inside the walls under
the label, *Breakfast Beef.* And more than a few of the
ranch-style homes within had their own stills. As
Hemingway viewed these homes, he contemplated
with pleasure his report to JCS that the largest oil
reserves in the world and its ARAMCO custodians
were again secure.

Beginning his descent over the softball diamond,
Hemingway spotted smoke and sucked in his breath
. . . "Damn!" he exclaimed. "What a fool I am.
God . . . damn!"

Jamming his throttle forward and throwing his
exhaust nozzles out of the vertical, he sped toward
the source of the smoke. Four homes were burning
close to a gate of the compound, and in the middle
of the street between the houses was an empty jeep
with a mounted machine gun.

He spotted two Saudi soldiers emerging from one
of the homes with a blonde woman in tow. For a
moment, Hemingway thought the soldiers had res-
cued her until they began ripping her robe off as
she struggled. A man, obviously hurt, lurched from
the same house before Hemingway could react.
Flinging the nude woman aside, the soldiers leveled
their Uzis at the man. Hemingway watched the
submachine guns jerk in the hands of the Saudis as
the man staggered backward into the house from

the force of their bullets. The blonde jumped up and ran toward the man.

Observing the woman a moment, the soldiers pointed their weapons at her back. Hemingway knew the crackling of the fires masked his engine noise from the soldiers, and he squeezed off a short volley of 25mm rounds to get their attention.

The heavy staccato of the Harrier's guns ripped the air above the soldiers, drawing their muzzles to the aircraft. After emptying their Uzis at the hovering plane, they ran to the jeep. The Saudis charged their vehicle toward the gate.

"Keep going . . . you yellow, sucking bastards," muttered Hemingway, easing the nose of his aircraft downward in pursuit.

When the jeep was clear of the burning homes, Hemingway flipped the HEAT switch on his weapons panel—activating a heat-seeking sensor on the tip of one of his Sidewinders. The sensor promptly registered the hot exhaust of the jeep by emitting an aural tone through the earphones of the Harrier's pilot. He squeezed his trigger.

White-hot flames shot from the tail of the five-inch-wide, 86-pound, nine-and-a-half-foot-long missile. It separated from Hemingway's wingtip and dropped toward the street as it homed in on its target.

The rocket's initial impact gave off a bright, white flash followed by an orange-red explosion that enveloped the jeep. Fragments flew out of the fireball, twisting in the air; and Hemingway saw the still intact front axle, its wheels aflame, sliding through the gate of the compound.

Keying his mike, Hemingway yelled, "Hammer, this is Gorilla 101! *Come in! Come in!*"

"Gorilla, this is—"

"Hemingway cut in. "Have the Russians returned?"

"Negative," replied Banks, "but F-18s from the Connie and Big E have—"

Interrupting again, Hemingway half-shouted, "The Saudis are murdering our people! Send a platoon of Marines into every American compound on the coast . . . *on the double!* My Harriers know where they are."

"On their way," responded Banks.

"And drop off a squad of Marines at the ARAMCO hospital," added Hemingway, thinking of Sandi, "to guard the Russian wounded." He pivoted in his hover and landed helicopter fashion beside the burning houses. Cutting his engine, Hemingway jumped to the street and sprinted to the home the blonde woman had re-entered.

Smoke poured from its door now, forcing him to crouch low in order to see inside. A few feet within the door, the naked woman was bent over her dead husband, arms locked around his torn, bloodied body. Flames ate at a rug beside the couple.

Hemingway crawled to them under the smoke. "Lady, is there anyone else in the house?"

She turned terror-stricken eyes to him and shook her head once. Over the roar of the flames, Hemingway cried out, "You've got to get out of here!"

The blonde fell upon her husband, fiercely renewing her grip. Reaching for her arm to ease the woman away from the body, Hemingway's hand slipped from her hot skin. A gust of smoke enveloped them as he placed his hands at her waist. He pulled gently, then harder when she still wouldn't let go. In the thickening smoke, Hemingway braced himself as he felt for her hipbones and yanked both the woman and her husband from the flames.

Their progress was halted at the door when the man's body became wedged in its opening. Hemingway attempted to loosen the woman's hands from her husband. Unable to break her death grip, he raised his fist to knock her unconscious but could no longer see the blonde's head through the swirling smoke.

In frustration and hopelessness, Hemingway opened his mouth to yell at her and got a lung full of acrid fumes instead. The blind and coughing Marine felt hands pulling him away from the house. He reached for the woman, but she was no longer there.

Halfway to the street where he could breathe again, Hemingway rasped, "The woman! Get the woman!"

As he struggled to his feet again, one of the men restraining him pointed down the sidewalk. "We got her, too!" shouted the man. At the curb, the soot-darkened woman still clutched her husband.

Recovering his senses, Hemingway told the men, "Get your cars out and barricade the gate!" As the three men ran to their garages, he climbed back into his cockpit and started his engine. This time, bringing the engine up as rapidly as possible, Hemingway was fully strapped in and had his exhaust nozzles at 10 degrees within 45 seconds. Stabilizing his engine at 55 percent, he moved his nozzles to 50 degrees and checked duct pressure—the pressure in tubes running to vents in his wingtips, nose, and tail through which engine air would be bled in order to stabilize the aircraft in vertical takeoff. A moment later, Hemingway moved the nozzles vertical and pushed his throttle to full power. In three seconds, the Harrier was thirty feet above the street.

Hemingway was barely over the housetops when he saw two open-bed, camouflaged trucks barreling down the highway parallel to the compound's wall. They were crammed with frenzied Saudi soldiers firing their weapons randomly into the air. Lowering his hover, Hemingway flipped on the HEAT switch again and moved forward. He saw the three American men who had blocked the compound gate with their cars walking down the street in his direction.

"Damn it!" swore Hemingway. "Get out of my way!" He released a burst of 25mm rounds over their heads and watched them scramble aside.

The first truck pulled into the entrance at high speed and bowled through the cars. The Harrier pilot again heard the aural tone in his earphones and pressed the trigger.

"Get in there, baby," he urged as another Sidewinder squirted off his wing and leaped forward.

The image of the truck disappeared a short moment in the blast of the rocket's impact, to be revealed again in a tangled mass of orange flames and fiery metal. Bringing his hover higher to pump 25mm rounds into the second truck, Hemingway recognized a flash from its rear.

"God, no!" he exclaimed.

Reacting instantly to the Stinger fired from the truck, Hemingway pushed his throttle to full power and with the thumb of the same hand selected his flare dispenser button. A canister dropped off the fuselage as the Harrier moved sluggishly higher.

He watched the heat-seeking missile surge toward him. It appeared to slow down by the force of his own concentration. At the last moment, the Stinger curved lower to seek out the white-hot ball of the magnesium flare, but this gave little comfort to the Marine pilot.

He waited for the buffet of the missile's detonation below him. It occurred at street level, little more than thirty feet from the belly of his Harrier. The slight thump it provided caused a temporary loss of stabilization as the plane yawed to port. This was followed by a low-pitched tone in this headset and flashing red gauges on the warning panel of his cockpit, telling Hemingway what he could already feel.

The decoy of the flare had only been a temporary escape. Shrapnel from the missile had penetrated and ignited fuel cells in his fuselage, in addition to damaging hydraulic and electrical lines. The engine ran rough, and his controls gave poor response as Hemingway fought to keep his aircraft near level. He knew he had only seconds to get out of the plane.

Cutting power, he put the Harrier into a controlled fall—the worst of learned options. There were no others. Ejection from the tilted aircraft had the potential of throwing him onto one of the burning homes to his rear. Better to ride it in and pray.

What're the soldiers going to do to those people? he thought. *I'll miss you, Sandi. Is my landing gear still down?* There was no time to pray.

King Khalid International Airport
Riyadh

"Your Highness," reported the Saudi general, "all units are in place."

Standing on the viewing platform atop the arch of the *royal* terminal at King Khalid International Airport, Prince Rahman and Crown Prince Saleem could see the tanks, mechanized vehicles, and soldiers clustered at the four corners of the airfield.

"How many Hawk and Stinger missiles are in each corner?" Rahman inquired of his general.

"Three truck-mounted Hawks and 20 Stingers, Your Highness. I have also placed 35 more Stingers on the roofs of hangars."

"Praise to Allah," replied Rahman. "And how many men at each corner of the runways?"

"A mobilized Land Force battalion, Your Highness." The officer added, "And units of the national guard are in reserve."

"My men have tasted blood," growled Prince Saleem, "and they want more."

This comment made little sense to Rahman, who had withhold the news that his men had also tasted blood—their own. The 32 Mirage-V fighters he'd sent to intercept the flight from South Yemen had fared worse than the F-15s over the Gulf. Officially, Rahman had reported half the Yemeni flight destroyed . . . with no losses among the Mirage-Vs. In fact, Rahman was uncertain *if any* of the planes from South Yemen had even been hit. He was certain of the fate of his Mirage-Vs. None had returned.

Two hundred fifty miles to the south, the Soviet flight commander issued instructions to Lieutenant Ivanoff. "Weasel 88, this is Drifter. I have received word the Saudis are defending the runways as expected. Wind-direction from the west. It is time for you to go."

"Spasibo, Drifter!" acknowledged Ivanoff buoyantly. He and seven other Fulcrums dove for ground level—stepping their speed up to Mach One—to avoid radar detection.

Colonel Romanov grinned at the lieutenant's reply. Ivanoff was a good choice. Few of the other fighter pilots in his command would have expressed gratitude for such a mission. Romanov did not report the earlier bombing of the runways, because his superiors had decided against informing their flight commanders of the American attacks.

The Fulcrums whipped past the landscape at fifty feet, the ground on either side and in front to a distance of 600 feet appearing only as a blur. Their shockwaves echoed across the desert floor, fracturing the eardrums of those caught within 2100 yards of their path. As a precaution to further mask their approach, the MiG pilots switched on their radars. At ground level, the MiG-29 radar was powerful enough to kill any mammal lower than the rabbit species within 1000 yards. The brains of higher mammals would be scrambled. Nearing Riyadh, the advance unit circled west to make their run.

The airfield in sight, Lieutenant Ivanoff barked: "Execute strike!" The eight MiG-29s paired off, each duo heading for a corner of the field. The fighters assigned to the eastern corners skirted around the western perimeter of the runways and increased their speed to Mach 1.6, which was barely enough to temporarily outrun any missiles launched by the ground forces.

As their fire-control computers locked onto the heat of the Saudi tanks and trucks, the Fulcrum pilots released their laser-controlled binary missiles and began evasive maneuvers.

Atop the royal terminal, the first indication of an attack was light-blue, billowing gas in the western corners of the airfield. Pointing to the west, Prince Rahman yelled to his chief of staff:. "What is that?"

The general snatched a military radio from the petrified soldier beside him and shouted the name of his commander in the northwest corner. "Colonel Hassan! Colonel Hassan!"

Even holding the radio receiver tightly to his ear, the general did not hear the choked rasp from Hassan's radioman as dual thunderclaps followed the first MiGs across the runways.

Alerted by the straining afterburners of the Soviet fighters, the Saudis frantically searched the skies for the source of the sound. As the MiGs were now covering a mile every three seconds (almost twice the speed of sound), only a few Saudis who looked far ahead of the ear-splitting roar and near ground level spotted the streaking MiG-29s. The Hawk missiles, pointed skyward, were useless against the low-flying planes.

Crown Prince Saleem peered at the western corners of the airfield through binoculars. "No one moves!" He thrust the glasses toward his half-brother.

Rahman watched through the magnifying lenses as the blue gas began to drift eastward. Except for a few motionless bodies on the ground, Colonel Hassan's command appeared deserted. Prince Rahman wheeled at Saleem's outcry.

"The eastern corners, *too*!"

The Saudi units in the east had disappeared in the same blue gas.

Glancing back over his target, Lieutenant Ivanoff shouted in alarm to his wingman. "Weasel 93! Missile on our six!"

The wingman veered sharp left and Ivanoff cut hard right. Viewing the corners of the airfield— each still wrapped in a bluish shroud—Ivanoff hit his UHF button to make his report. "Drifter, this is Wea—"

A tracking Stinger slipped up the exhaust of his MiG-29, splitting the fuselage. Knocked unconscious, Ivanoff felt nothing as a second missile exploded on the front half of his plane.

An Englishman wearing a mobile headset appeared at Rahman's side. "Your Highness, the Control Tower reports a large flight of unidentified aircraft approaching from the southwest."

"How soon do they arrive?" Rahman asked.

The Englishman checked his watch. "Fourteen minutes."

In seconds, the Englishman was the only one still standing on the viewing platform as Rahman, Saleem, and their staffs jammed the elevators and stairs leading from the arch. At the main floor of the terminal, they raced toward the exits. Scores of Saudi civilians who were at the broad windows facing the runways turned to watch the panicked soldiers.

"*Save yourselves*!" shrieked one of the Land Force officers. "The Russians come!"

The men at the windows stared after the officer as he pushed his way out a door. A few of the civilians started for the exits before the momentary silence was broken by a Saudi dressed in a cream-colored Western-style suit.

"Save Saudi Arabia!" he passionately cried out. Then even louder: "In the Name of Allah, SAVE SAUDI ARABIA!"

Most of the Saudis moving toward the exits paused as the young man in the light suit jumped onto a ticket counter and fiercely declared:

"I am *Hamud bin Abdul Aziz Al Saud!*"

The others recognized at once the youngest and most profligate son of the late founder of their kingdom. Prince Hamud glowered at those below as he snarled, "And I will not leave like a crawling dog."

The few Saudis still moving froze in their tracks at the taunt.

"Who will be the first," Hamud challenged, "to smash a Russian plane with his car?"

"In the Name of Allah," a young Saudi in traditional thobe shouted back, "*I will!*"

Hamud acknowledged his cousin with a raised fist. "Only if you are swifter than I, Prince Karrim! *To our cars!* We shall see who will be first!"

Hamud leaped from the counter, grabbed Irene's sleeve, and ran to an exit . . . followed by the

young men in his audience. Outside, most of the
military vehicles were now gone, as were many of
the civilian cars. Releasing Irene at his convertible,
Hamud jumped over the driver's door and switched
on the ignition. When he looked up, Irene still stood
by her door.

"Let's go!" Hamud yelled.

She shook her head. "I'm not going with you."

"Don't worry," he smiled reassuringly. "The
Russians won't land when they see cars blocking
the runways."

"You're out of your mind," snapped Irene.

Hamud yelled back: "Do you want to stay *here?*"

Urgently glancing around, Irene saw no Westerners—only Saudi men, a few of whom eyed her as
if waiting to see whether Hamud would leave her
behind. Irene got into the car.

As they snaked in and out of the traffic, Hamud
reached over to touch her arm. "I need your
dress," he said.

Irene's eyes opened wide. "What?"

His expression was dead-serious. "I will give you
ten thousand dollars for it."

This solicited an even more bewildered look from
Irene.

"Fifty thousand!" Hamud impatiently offered.

"Why?"

"It is *green,*" he declared. "The color of the Saudi flag."

She shook her head in disbelief.

"Please," he urged. *"One hundred thousand dollars."*

Still shaking her head, Irene reached under the
thobe to remove the dress. When she handed it

over, Hamud began waving it high over his head as he drove.

The cacophony of horns behind them trebled.

Agitated at his slow pace, Hamud abruptly pulled his car onto the long passenger island and blared his horn to clear off the pedestrians as he accelerated down his newly created lane. He was followed by a tight line of Mercedes, Cadillacs, BMWs, assorted limousines, and several European sports cars. With his green standard held high in the air, Hamud led his procession from the terminal area and swung onto a transition road leading to the parking lot where he'd left his Lear Jet.

At its gate, Hamud slammed on his brakes. The iron-barred gate was locked and the Pakistani guard gone. Backing up, Hamud told Irene to buckle up her seatbelt as he aligned the white Rolls directly at the center of the barrier. Hamud didn't bother with his seatbelt.

He floored his gas pedal. On contact, his head pitched forward and bounced off the steering wheel as the gate halted the charging convertible. Bleeding slightly from his forehead, Hamud threw his car in reverse again and gunned it backward. Handing Irene the dress, he snapped on his seat belt and directed the two nearest Saudi drivers to charge with him. Hamud pointed a black Mercedes limo to the middle position. When they were aligned, Hamud screamed, "Allah Akbar!"

Out of unison, the cars leaped forward, failing to hit the barrier together. On the next try, they bowled over the pillar holding the gate and burst into the parking lot.

When the Saudis still in the terminal saw the

madly weaving caravan led by a white convertible flying a green standard, many of them also ran to their vehicles to join the foray.

Prince Hamud halted in the middle of the airfield and stood atop the hood of his car. From this vantage point, he directed cars to patrol all of the runways as Irene worriedly scanned the skies.

ARAMCO

The blurred figure above Hemingway gradually became clearer. He recognized the distinctive earphones of a Sea Stallion pilot before the man's face fully registered.

"Coming to, Doc," announced the helicopter pilot.

The Navy corpsman kneeled at Hemingway's side.

"What happened?" asked Hemingway, his jaw movement dislodging the petrolatum gauze over his left cheek. The resulting pain kept him from saying more.

Repositioning the gauze, the medic placed Hemingway's hand over it. "Colonel, hold your bandage in place and don't try to talk."

When the searing agony of his cheek subsided, Hemingway's eyes opened again and scrutinized the corpsman who'd ordered him quiet. The corpsman scowled back.

"You've got third-degree burns over the entire left side of your face, Colonel. It'll hurt like hell again if you let the gauze fall off." The medic took a syringe from his packet and removed the cap covering its needle. He plunged the needle deep into the biceps muscle of the pilot.

Hemingway jerked his arm away, and most of the crystal-clear fluid in the syringe spurted into the air.

"No drugs!" snapped the Marine colonel.

"It's just morphine," protested the corpsman.

"No drugs," repeated Hemingway, feeling drowsy already from the minor dosage he'd received. Grimacing as he spoke, Hemingway switched his attention to the Sea Stallion pilot.

"What happened?" he demanded again.

"After you crash-landed," replied the lieutenant, "the people here broke through your canopy with their tire irons and pulled you out."

"Where're the Saudis?"

The lieutenant grinned. "They turned tail when they saw my Stallion coming in." He added, "I spotted the flash of your 'Winder and came in fast."

Disapproval clouded Hemingway's face at the thought that the escaping Saudis might return with reinforcements.

"Relax, sir," said the lieutenant, reading the frown. "The Saudis won't be back. One of our PBLs accidentally sliced into the fuel tank of their truck."

The medic leaned over Hemingway. "I've got to get back to the others, Colonel. They're worse off than you."

"These people were sure determined to get you out of that Harrier," commented the lieutenant. "Two of them lost all their hair and most of their clothes."

Holding the petrolatum-saturated gauze to his cheek, Hemingway attempted to raise himself to his elbows and nearly passed out from the pain of his effort. He collapsed, squeezing his eyes shut and breathing heavily.

"What's wrong, sir?"

Hemingway whispered, "My back."

"Probably jammed it hitting the deck, Colonel. I'll tell the medic."

"Forget that," Hemingway told him sharply. "Take me to the Norlin house."

The lieutenant raised his brow in concern. "Sir, we've already called in another helo to take you to the hospital."

The Marine lieutenant colonel slowly repeated himself. "Take me to the Norlin house first."

"I don't think that's wise, sir," persisted the lieutenant. "Your back may be broken."

"Goddamn it!" blustered Hemingway, wincing at his aching face, "as long as I can breathe, *I'm* in command around here!"

The junior officer hesitated.

"Follow my orders, Marine!" Hemingway threatened, "Or I'll have your ass court-martialed!"

The lieutenant jumped to his feet. "I'll be right back, sir." He returned with a civilian, the two of them carrying a narrow plywood panel. Against the Navy corpsman's objections, they slid Hemingway onto it and placed him in the back of a station wagon.

At the Norlin house, Hemingway asked to be taken into the room with the ham radio. As they carried him through the hallway, he saw the horrified faces of Dori and Kevin gaping down at the large, raised blisters covering his reddened, hairless scalp. The two children followed Hemingway into

Kevin's bedroom where the open-mouthed boy managed to speak.

"What happened to *you*?"

"A little accident," replied the pilot, looking away from the repulsive expression on the boy's face. "Kids, I need your help. Do you have any friends in the States with ham radios?"

The twins exchanged glances. "She has one in Florida," replied Kevin, "and I have one in Philadelphia."

"I want you to reach one of them. Whomever you get first, tell them to contact the White House in my name—Colonel Thomas Hemingway."

Dori sat down before the radio, put on the headset, hit several switches, and began working the dials.

"Kevin," said Hemingway, "is there a mirror around here?"

The boy brought a small vanity mirror to the bed.

After checking his scalp, the pilot lifted the protective gauze from a corner of his cheek. A section of beet-red skin came away with the gauze, exposing raw-meaty flesh, white tendons, and open blood vessels. A dime-sized portion of his left ear had melted away. Handing the mirror back to Kevin, Hemingway shut his eyes and listened as Dori repeated her call sign. After several fruitless minutes, she turned the radio over to her brother. Kevin had no better luck.

"There's no answer from either of our friends," declared Dori. "We usually write before calling them, so they'll know when to listen."

"Keep trying," Hemingway told her. "We've

got to get through to them." As she moved out of his line of vision, he added, "Try to reach anyone . . . as long as they're in the States."

Kevin surrendered the radio's headset back to his sister, who rotated the dials again and listened for English without a British accent. Hemingway had fallen asleep when she cried out, *"I've got someone!"* Hitting several switches to fine-tune, she pulled the mike before her and spoke excitedly.

"Break! This is SA8ADN . . . this is SA8ADN!"

Hearing the rare Middle East call sign, a ham operator in Bangor, Maine promptly broke off her Stateside call to respond.

"SA8ADN," responded the woman, "this is NA1DGH. Do you copy? Over."

"NA1DGH, this is SA8ADN. I read you loud and clear. I have emergency traffic. Can you handle it? Over."

"SA8ADN, what is the nature of your emergency traffic? Over."

Dori smiled at Hemingway. "NA1DGH, I have a military message for the White House. Over."

The voice of the woman from Maine turned shrill. "SA8ADN, *get off* this frequency! Go find someone else to play with, young lady?"

Hemingway called out, "Let me talk to her!" Dori extended the microphone to him.

He took the mike and set it on his chest. "This is Colonel Thomas Hemingway of the United States Marines speaking. I am in Saudi Arabia and it is imperative that I get a message to the White House as soon as possible. Will you help me?"

The woman's voice was still skeptical. "Why are you using a ham radio if you're in the military?"

"I'm at the ARAMCO compound in eastern Saudi Arabia," he replied, "and our normal communications have been knocked out or jammed. Who and where are you?"

"Lisa Hill," she answered hesitantly. "Bangor, Maine."

"Fine, Miss Hill. Now will you contact the White House for me?"

"It's *Mrs.* Hill," she corrected. After a pause, she replied, "Even if I believed you, I doubt if anyone at the White House would believe *me.*"

"Just try," pleaded Hemingway. "Tell them Colonel Hemingway of the U.S.S. Puller wishes to speak with the President."

The woman replied without enthusiasm. "I'll try . . . once. Stand by."

The long-distance operator surprised her by getting an immediate connection. Then again, it was late.

"Hello, this is the White House," announced a formal woman's voice.

Mrs. Hill swallowed. "Hello . . . I'm calling from Maine, and I have a Marine officer on my ham radio who wants to communicate with the President."

"I'm sorry, ma'am," came the quick and aloof reply, "we cannot connect you with the President. Would you care to leave a message?"

"Well . . . yes. A Colonel Hemingway in Saudi Arabia wishes to talk with the President. He has some communications problem."

"I have your message," the operator replied impatiently. "Thank you for calling."

"Wait a minute!" cried out Mrs. Hill. "You don't have my phone number yet."

The operator's tone became curt. "I'll take it if you wish, ma'am."

"It's 809-8593, area code 209."

"Very well, ma'am, *Goodbye.*"

Hearing the disconnect, Mrs. Hill muttered, "Goodbye to you, too . . . bitch."

King Khalid International Airport Riyadh

"There they are!" cried Irene, pointing to the northwest. Hamud slipped behind the steering wheel of the Rolls and hit his horn to alert the others . . . keeping an eye on the lone MiG preceding the Russian flight.

Making a high pass over the runways, the Soviet commander saw that Lieutenant Ivanoff's strike had been deadly accurate. No missiles or anti-aircraft fire climbed to greet him. The cars scampered like mice across the airfield but failed to impress Colonel Romanov until scores of them converged behind his flight path. Sensing their purpose, he hit his UHF button.

"Weasels, this is Drifter. Descend and clear the runways." Romanov then ordered his Ilyushins to circle at 3000 meters, an error he wouldn't realize until debriefed by superiors.

In their initial runs, the MiGs knocked out a quarter of the Saudi cars—most of whom foolishly tried to outrun the fighters in headlong sprints. When the cars began circling at high speed, the MiG pilots were less successful and had destroyed only a few more when the careless pilots of two planes collided. As the pair of MiGs exploded on the tarmac, Romanov depressed his UHF button.

"Weasels, this is Drifter. Enough of this play! Marshall at 4000 meters."

The Saudis blared their horns in triumph as Prince Hamud sped across the airfield in an attempt to evenly distribute the remaining cars.

Altering his original plan, Colonel Romanov issued instructions to his first Ilyushin. "Ghost 216, you will land at the east end of the northernmost runway. Weasels 72, 74, 76, and 78 will clear your path."

When the single transport with its fighter escort circled down to the field, most of the Saudi drivers left their assigned areas to charge the intruders, and the 20mm cannon of the MiGs tore a wide swath through those cars which accurately anticipated the touchdown point of the Ilyushin. Most of the drivers, however, drove directly at the in-flight transport and quickly trailed behind it, remaining relatively untouched by the MiGs and unseen by the transport pilot. Seeing the danger, Romanov barked another order. "Weasels, 62, 64, 66, and 68. Clean up the Ilyushin's rear!"

As the main wheel mounts of the transport made contact with the concrete, a brown Maserati swept under its tail and aimed for the eight-tire wheel mount beneath its left wing. Coming in at 140 miles per hour, the car bounced off the massive tires, yet the impact still blew the four rear tires of the mount. The reduced port traction caused the Ilyushin to veer right before its pilot added power to his starboard engine to maintain a semblance of direction.

Adjusting his port throttles to three-quarters, the Ilyushin pilot reversed the turbo-fans of his engines as a gray Jaguar angled in toward the already-damaged wheel mount. Traveling much faster than the slowing transport, the car sheered off the mount, causing the tip of the left wing to slam to the tarmac.

Trailing a hail of sparks, the plane spun sharply to the left and after three revolutions came to a halt. Dark-complexioned soldiers burst from the hatches of its fuselage, formed a tight circle around their plane, and began firing upon the cars. The Saudi drivers drove in irregular patterns about the Ilyushin and became easy prey for the diving Fulcrums . . . until they followed the lead of the white convertible flying a green standard from its antenna. Hamud and Irene were weaving a wide circle around the downed aircraft.

Four thousand feet above, Romanov waited anxiously for the ramp of the Ilyushin to drop and deliver its cargo. When no tank appeared within a reasonable time, he hit his UHF mike button.

"Ghost 216, this is Drifter. *Drop* your ramp!"

"It doesn't open," came the reply. "The landing jammed it." The transport pilot's attention was drawn elsewhere.

A blue-and-silver Porsche had broken inside the weaving circle and made a beeline for the nose wheel of his Ilyushin. The ring of soldiers at the front of the plane parted for the speeding car, which swerved from the nose wheel at the last moment, clipping the nose mount with its rearend. The weakened mount slowly bent from the vertical and collapsed, plopping the nose of the Ilyushin to the tarmac as the out-of control Porsche rolled, throwing the driver into the air. The body twitched on the concrete as it was saturated by the bullets of the soldiers.

A cherry-red Ferrari turned in next from the circling cars and accelerated directly at the nose of the Ilyushin. As the soldiers peppered the Ferrari, the pilot and copilot of the plane tore at their seat belts. Twenty yards from the nose, the Ferrari driver opened his door and rolled out.

The fuselage shuddered slightly at the impact of the car, and its nose erupted in flames. A Bedouin sheik saw the driver of the Ferrari lying motionless in a face-down position and punched the intercom to his chauffeur. "Drive between the plane and the driver of the red car!" ordered the sheik.

The pink and chrome limousine instantly cut inside, and bullets whanged off its armored frame and windows as it screeched to a halt beside the prone body. When the Bedouin jumped from his door to rescue his countryman, the Ferrari driver popped up and dove inside the car. Stepping to the front door of his Continental, the sheik yanked his chauffeur out and pointed him into the rear seat.

The Bedouin tromped on his gas pedal. Instead of returning to the circle of cars, he turned toward the plane. Paralleling the fuselage, the limousine plowed through its defenders. When it returned to the band of cars, one soldier's body partially blocked its windshield and two more hung from its grill.

A slew of Saudis promptly left the circle and darted for the other side of the fuselage. The first of the cars to attack received heavy fire, and few of the drivers succeeded in their quest. Other cars, as they neared the side of the plane, twisted in tight curves in an effort to pick off their own trophies.

The cordon of cars around the Ilyushin soon dissolved as all the Saudis charged the burning plane in the contest to drag off its defenders. Before the soldiers retreated under the fuselage and onto the downed wing, more than a few of the Saudi drivers carried off proof of their courage.

Losing their targets, the cars reformed in a tighter ring about the plane to avoid the MiGs. The Saudis were now content to let the fire complete their work.

Prince Karrim—having clipped several soldiers with his BMW, yet having no proof of his prowess—cut inside and sped toward the tip of the downed wing. Freezing his brakes just before the wingtip, he released them the instant before his front wheels made contact. The car jumped onto the wing and Karrim floored the accelerator. The soldiers who had sought refuge on the left wing scattered off as he raced toward the fuselage. Where both wings met at the top of the fuselage. Karrim continued his charge and crossed over to the starboard side. Completely surprising the soldiers on this wing, the BMW spilled them off like dominoes.

From far above, Colonel Romanov watched a small car sail off the upright wing of the downed Ilyushin before crashing on its side. The Russian flight commander swore to himself. "For every bastard we kill, five crazier bastards take his place!" Punching his UHF button, he announced, "Weasels, disengage and return to Marshall."

Later, there would be little dispute among the participants on the runways of King Khalid International Airport that the driver of the BMW had executed the finest charge of the day.

For a short time, the surviving soldiers huddled under the fuselage and delivered an ineffective fire on the cars. When the heat from the burning plane became unbearable, the Ilyushin crew and soldiers dropped their weapons and tried to move away from the flames with raised hands. They were shown no mercy.

As the brief contest came to a close, Hamud and Irene extricated the injured Karrim from his crushed BMW. His proud grin beamed through a face streaming with blood.

"Praise to Allah," he said. "Only my arm is broken."

After staunching the flow of blood from his split scalp, they placed Karrim in their backseat and returned to the middle of the field with a few of the other cars. Most of the Saudis charged haphazardly about the runways, again blasting their horns in triumph.

"Another comes!" pointed Hamud to the same northern runway. As the Ilyushin glided down, Irene checked far above and behind the transport.

"Where're the MiGs?" she asked.

"Wait!" called Hamud to the Saudis who'd joined him at midfield. They watched the other drivers chase after the new prize.

"Ghost 222, this is Drifter," announced the Russian flight commander. "Commence touchdown."

The transport pilot gunned his engines to push ahead of the slower cars and descended to the tarmac. The trailing drivers frantically raced each other for the honor of being first to cripple the second plane. After touching the runway, the Ilyushin went to full throttle and became airborne. It touched down again at half-mile intervals farther down the runway. And each time, the Saudi drivers charged en masse.

"They are fools!" exclaimed Prince Karrim. With the hand of his good arm, he directed their attention to the southeast. "Look to the *smoke!"* At a height of thirty feet, an Ilyushin skimmed over the desert toward the airfield, trailed by twelve Fulcrums belching black smoke at their reduced speeds.

Colonel Romanov smiled at the seven cars speeding south. The Ilyushin's tank would make short work of any drivers who got through his Fulcrums. He pressed his UHF button. "Weasels in the south, this is Drifter. The mice come."

When the drivers of the seven cars spotted the ground-level MiGs coming directly at them in the distance, they spread wider, which only served to give the MiG pilots better target selection. The cars swerved from side to side as they increased speed.

The fighter pilots, approaching in three sections, had already selected the HEAT buttons of their fire-control computers. Getting aural tones, the first section of four MiGs released their missiles and watched the four nearest cars disintegrate moments later. Hamud thanked Allah his Rolls-Royce was slower than the others as he dodged the burning pieces of fragmented vehicles.

The second section of MiGs released their missiles seconds after the first wave, and the third section followed in unison. Standard operating procedure for the pilots would have been to climb abruptly to avoid target debris, but their orders were to promptly regroup around the landing Ilyushin.

As the relatively slow-moving MiGs banked right and left low to the ground, the missiles fired by the second and third waves curved away from the surviving cars in pursuit of the greater sources of heat. By the time radar scans in the first two sections of MiGs reported tracking missiles, evasive action from the supersonic rockets was out of the question. A few of the pilots chose their first instinct and yanked ejection handles—another hopeless option. With their aircraft banking in tight turns, these pilots rode their seats out of their cockpits toward the horizon and cartwheeled along the concrete runways at speeds exceeding 80 miles per hour, separating from their seats in the process. Those pilots who took longer to think had their fate decided for them as the exhausts of their Fulcrums sucked up the missiles fired by the other MiGs. The stunned pilots in the third section circled after the Saudi drivers, reaching the cars as the Ilyushin touched down.

Hamud and Irene, accompanied by a Clenet and Lamborghini, were 150 yards from the transport's port side when 20mm cannon fire began ricocheting off the runway beside them. The Clenet burst into flames, and the Lamborghini suddenly swerved right, forcing Hamud to jerk his wheel away from the second vehicle. Regaining control of his car, Hamud felt a hot, stabbing pain in his left shoulder and saw pieces of blood-stained, cream-colored cloth splatter across the dashboard in front of him.

Hamud's left hand went limp, falling uselessly

from the steering wheel. Feeling the strength ebbing from his right arm as well, he whirled to Irene. She stared in shock at the bone splinters, spongy body tissue, and blood dripping off the burled wood of the dash.

"Steer!" Hamud cried out.

Holding a scream, Irene seized the wheel.

"Under the plane!" howled Prince Karrim. "Under the plane! They cannot shoot us there!"

Irene pulled herself across the seat and maneuvered the car below a wing of the aircraft. Keeping pace with its shadow, she was uncertain what to do next. Thinking to alarm the transport's pilot, she repeatedly pounded the horn. With great effort, Hamud raised his right hand and pointed to the wheel mount at the nose of the jet.

"Hit it," he weakly commanded.

Controlled by her fear, Irene could not react.

"Steer!" Hamud cried again. He jammed his foot over hers and floored the gas pedal. Prepared to die, Hamud stiffened and closed his eyes.

Irene let go her scream as the car came up on the wheel mount.

Hamud felt no impact and wondered if he was in heaven. He mumbled, "Praise to Allah." He opened his eyes and watched the image of the Ilyushin grow smaller as he slipped into unconsciousness.

Colonel Romanov hit his UHF button. "Tikonov, *what are you doing?"* he shrieked. "Get back on the ground!"

For a long moment, the transport's pilot did not respond. When he did, it was in a low, tense voice.

"I cannot land, Drifter."

Romanov bellowed back, "*Why the hell not?*"

"I have no choice."

"Damn you, Tikonov!" bellowed Romanov in frustration. "Get back down!"

Observing the confusion below, the pilots and troop commanders in the circling Ilyushins listened intently to the strange exchange. The lone transport continued to climb and left the perimeter of the airfield with its remaining MiG escorts.

"If I attempt to land again," Tikonov explained, "I shall be shot, just—"

"I'll shoot you down myself," Romanov interrupted, "if you *do not!*"

"The Cubans have killed my copilot," Tikonov responded. "They now hold a gun to *my head.*"

"That is not possible!" howled the Russian flight commander.

A Cuban officer listening to the conversation through the headset of the dead copilot coolly replied, "Comrade Colonel, you promised our landings would be unopposed. This is not true. Therefore, I have ordered my plane to return to Yemen."

"*You yellow dog!*" screamed Romanov. "I'll have you shot if you return to Yemen."

"We will see *who* is to be shot, comrade," scoffed the Cuban.

"But your plane had a chance," Romanov desperately argued.

"For how long?" hissed the Cuban officer. "Your fighters could not even protect the first transport. They are better at shooting down their own. My men never had a chance."

On the airfield below, dozens of Saudi cars patrolled the southern runways, having realized the Soviet ploy. Colonel Romanov could say or do nothing to dissuade the Cubans in the other Ilyushins from also heading south to safety.

The White House

After scribbling the message on a memo, the operator placed it in a dispatch box above her console. Fifteen minutes later, a clerk collected all the messages in the switchboard room and deposited them in the routing office.

Sorting through several hundred messages, the router pulled twenty-six of them for forwarding and discarded the balance. Three of the messages were marked ''rush,'' including Hemingway's. The router then pressed a buzzer to summon a courier. In this manner the message from Bangor reached the presidential assistant in the War Room forty minutes after it arrived at the White House.

Upon examining the memo, Hoolihan offered it to the President. ''Sir, would you like me to contact this lady?''

President Steiner scanned it and picked up the phone himself. ''This is the President. Put me through to 209-555-8593.'' When the telephone started to ring, he transferred the call to the speaker box on the conference table and sat down.

Lisa Hill skeptically answered, ''Hello.''

''Are you the person who just called the White House?'' asked the President.

167

"Yes," she hesitantly replied. "About an hour ago."

"This is President Steiner, Mrs. Hill. Can you tell me how you obtained the name of Colonel Hemingway?"

"Is this *actually the President?*" she queried.

He laughed good-naturedly. "Yes, Mrs. Hill. Now, please tell me how you heard from Colonel Hemingway?"

"He interrupted me on my ham radio."

"Is he still on it?"

"Hold on," she responded. "I'll check."

General Steel addressed the President. "Sir, if she'll tell us what frequency her radio's on, we may be able to establish direct communication with Hemingway."

The President nodded, waiting for the woman to return. "He's still there," she finally replied.

"Thank you, Mrs. Hill. Would you mind telling me what frequency your ham radio's on?"

"Fourteen point one seven zero megahertz."

"Fine," said the President. "Did Colonel Hemingway have any messages for me?"

"He told me earlier that there was a war going on over in Saudi Arabia. Hold on while I check with him again."

After a lengthy interval, she returned. "President Steiner, I'm sorry it took so long. I had to make a list of what he told me. Here it is:

Landing from the east repulsed. Have 142 Soviet prisoners, and a body count of 289 more. 138 killed by Saudis and balance from plane crash. U.S.S. Puller sunk by Saudi gunboat. MAU commander and 7 others dead,

24 wounded. No Marine casualties at Dhahran. Request instructions for Russian POWs.

That's his message," she concluded.

"*Thank you,* Mrs. Hill," gushed the President. "Thank you very much indeed. Please tell Colonel Hemingway we'll respond shortly."

"After I tell him that, I'm going next door to get some help."

The President paused. "Why do you need help?"

"I can't be two places at once. My ham radio's about sixty feet from this telephone."

President Steiner kept his tone cordial. "I'd prefer, for security purposes, to minimize the number of people on this line, Mrs. Hill."

"Oh, don't worry about that," she quickly added. "I was only going to get my sister . . . she doesn't gossip with anyone but me."

"Okay," the President half-smiled, "but hurry back, please." Hearing the phone contact a countertop, the President surveyed the faces around the conference table. "Well, gentlemen, we did it. We lost some men, but we did it."

Hoolihan nodded his head. "Congratulations, sir."

"Thanks, Jim. I'd like you to go upstairs and inform the Congressmen that the Russians have been turned back at Dhahran, and we have 142 prisoners. Don't reveal more than that."

General Steel extended his hand. "My compliments, sir."

"Thank you, Bob," grinned the President. "Now, what do we do with the prisoners?" Before anyone could respond, he added quizzically, "And what happened to the Puller?"

The general pondered both questions a moment. "We'll find out soon enough about the Puller, I imagine. Concerning the prisoners, I'd suggest their immediate evacuation from Saudi Arabia . . . if we wish to maintain control over them."

As he listened to his general, the President was bemused that he'd requested a military opinion first. Without looking at his secretary of state, he said, "Clayton, what do you think?"

"Under international law, we have no jurisdiction over them. They belong to the Saudis." Walters paused a moment. "But leaving them in Saudi Arabia might encourage the Soviets to attempt a rescue mission . . . or another invasion under that guise. I would eliminate that risk and therefore concur with General Steel."

"The next question," the President stated, "is how to evacuate them and to where."

Steel offered, "Our helicopters at Dhahran could take them to Oman, and from there they could be transferred to our carriers."

"The helicopters would have to refuel on the way," injected the Marine Commandant.

"Where?" asked Clayton Walters pointedly.

Huering studied the Middle East wall grid. "Somewhere within the United Arab Emirates."

I'd advise against the helicopters then," asserted Walters. "The leaders in both the Emirates and Oman are even less predictable than the Saudis. If we lost control of the POWs in either country, the results could be grievous."

General Huering broke the resulting silence. "Why not bring the Connie into the Gulf?"

President Steiner watched frowns of disapproval light up among the other military men at the conference table.

"That's a two-billion dollar gamble," declared Steel.

"I agree," Huering nodded, "but I was also considering the deterrent effect a carrier battle group would pose. We don't know what's happening to the Soviet flight coming into Riyadh. If it succeeds in gaining a foothold, the Connie's presence might help us contain them."

Knowing what he intended to do, President Steiner addressed Admiral Sparks. "What's your position, Admiral?"

"Sir, I agree with General Steel." The President's expression hardened to a scowl as Sparks continued. "Pulling the Connie into the Gulf would be a brash move. However, at this moment, I don't know of a better option if we want to show the Russians we mean business."

The President's expression almost changed to one of relief . . . but the last words he'd heard jogged his memory. A scant two hours earlier, he had relieved a general who'd spoken the same words. Now, he himself *was considering them.*

"Then we do it," announced the President. "Bob, issue the necessary orders."

"It is vital," interjected Admiral Sparks firmly, "that the F-18s belonging to the Enterprise return to her, so she can provide cover for the Connie. The Enterprise can do so by taking up a station just south of the Strait of Hormuz."

"A relay of F-18s," added Huering, "could also keep us apprised of what's happening in the Gulf until the jamming stops."

President Steiner nodded affirmatively. "Instruct our communications people to resume coding messages, Bob. The Russians don't need to know what we're doing now."

Jim Hoolihan returned to the War Room and approached the President. "Sir, the congressmen asked me to convey their concern that the Soviet prisoners be repatriated without delay."

President Steiner made a grim smile. "They sound scared."

Hoolihan nodded.

"So am I," continued the President. "We're not out of this yet." He stood to pick up the open line to the ham radio in Bangor. "Hello? Mrs. Hill?"

"Hi!" came the shrill reply. It was a child's voice.

The President held his phone away for a moment to study it. "Who is this?" he hesitantly asked.

"Chris—ti—na," the girl proudly drew out.

"And who are you?" President Steiner inquired uncertainly.

"I'm a girl, silly?" The child giggled with delight, believing the man's words were a joke.

The man's words became serious. "Is this the Hill residence?"

The child paused. "What?"

"Is this Mrs. Hill's house?"

Another longer pause. "You mean Aunt Lee?" the girl asked.

"Yes . . . your Aunt Lee. May I speak to her?"

"Aunt Lee?" Her amplified voice carried throughout the War Room as the President pushed the phone out to arm's length to protect his ears.

"Hello," said the girl's aunt.

"There you are," sighed the President. "Would you give Colonel Hemingway this message? Prisoners are to be evacuated to the Constellation, but safeguard them for now. We'll send details soon."

The woman's voice went lower. "I was just talking to him, and he asked me to tell you that Saudi Arabian soldiers have killed Americans in the ARAMCO compound."

A sharp, electrical shock paralyzed the President's legs, and the constriction in his veins forced him to throw out a hand to the conference table to steady himself.

"How many, Mrs. Hill? Ask him how many."

"He's already told me. Five for sure, and maybe more in some houses they burnt down. He also said to tell you that Marines have been sent into all American compounds in eastern Saudi Arabia."

Restored somewhat, President Steiner thanked her and thought to ask of the young girl. "By the way, who's Christina?"

"That's my five-year-old niece. Her mother had to stay with her sick baby, so she sent Christina over to watch the phone. No one believes I'm actually talking to you, sir . . . ah, Mr. President."

"That's just fine, Mrs. Hill. For the time being, let's keep it that way. Now, could you ask Colonel Hemingway to tell us what he knows of the Puller's sinking?"

Dhahran Airbase

Eighty miles west of Dhahran Air Base, the F-15 fighters escorting the Saudi king from Riyadh picked up approaching F-18 Hornets on their radarscans. The two Saudi fighters came up tighter on the embassy helicopter for their own protection. When the helicopter touched down beside the Control Tower at Dhahran, the F-15s landed closeby and taxied toward it.

Louis Fricke alighted from the helicopter as a jeep carrying three Marines pulled up. He addressed the officer in the jeep. "Where's your CO, Lieutenant?"

"Hop in, sir. I'll take you to him." The lieutenant slipped to the rear of the jeep. After Fricke settled into the front seat, the driver twisted the wheel and reversed direction.

"Wait!" shouted Fricke. He scrutinized the two Saudi F-15s now approaching the helicopter. "Lieutenant, can you blow their tires?"

"Now?"

"Now!" repeated Fricke.

"The PBL, Corporal."

The Marine in the rear seat aimed a suitcase-shaped weapon and pressed its activator. A silent and intense ray of red emitted from the short, squared muzzle of the weapon. Fricke's eyes followed the line of the laser to the nosewheel of the nearest Saudi fighter.

"How's that, sir?" inquired the lieutenant smugly.

The nosewheel became a soft mass of jellied rubber. The plane still managed to move forward, turning slowly in the direction of the jeep as the PBL melted its other tires.

"That's not stopping them!" Fricke shouted.

The Saudi pilot released a burst of 20mm rounds to the front of the jeep.

"On his flank!" howled the lieutenant, yanking the XRL off the driver's shoulder. The jeep swung around to a position thirty-five yards beside the aircraft as the lieutenant leveled the new weapon.

Fricke impatiently watched the muzzle of the XRL. Seeing a cobalt blue beam spurt from the weapon, he shifted his attention to the F-15. Its nose suddenly appeared out of focus. As the entire plane became an agitated blur, its left wing loosened and clattered to the tarmac, followed by a bright flash. The F-15 became engulfed in flames. A split second later, the men in the jeep observed the Saudi pilot and his seat rocketing out of the plane to a height of about one hundred feet above the ground. At the apex of the ejection, the seat separated from the pilot whose parachute blossomed above him. He yanked frantically on his shroud lines to keep from drifting toward the flaming remains of his aircraft.

"Damn," muttered Fricke.

The Marine officer aimed the weapon at the other fighter.

"Hold it!" yelled Fricke.

The cockpit canopy of the second F-15 had popped up. Its pilot stretched his hands high above his head where they remained until the Marines approached and removed him from his aircraft.

After receiving a brief description of the action at Dhahran and ARAMCO from Colonel Banks, the embassy party reboarded their helicopter and were escorted by a Sea Stallion to ARAMCO. Banks radioed ahead and they were met at the softball field by John Norlin. The Saudi king still carried the child, now wrapped in a field jacket provided by a Marine.

As they silently crowded into the bedroom—the one with the ham radio—Ambassador Clark studied the disfigured head of the sleeping pilot a moment. Dori sat on the edge of the bed holding the bandage to his face.

"Is that Colonel Hemingway?" whispered Clark.

John Norlin nodded. "His plane crash-landed defending us from two truck loads of Saudi national guard. He told me to wake him when you arrived." Norlin nudged the pilot's arm.

Hemingway opened his eyes and gazed at the newcomers.

"I'm Emory Clark," began the ambassador, stepping forward. He motioned behind him. "This is King Asad and my Air Force attache, Major Fricke." The Royal Guard officer and Korean waited by the door.

After his head cleared, Hemingway explained, "The morphine they gave me keeps knocking me out." Scrutinizing the Saudi king, he asked the ambassador. "Why'd you leave Riyadh?"

Clark described the events at the embassy and at the Lockheed compound. Taking it in, Hemingway bitterly glared at Asad before speaking.

"I wonder why Washington forgot to inform the Marines that the national guard decided not to co-operate? It cost us more lives here, too . . . plus our ship."

Clark shook his head. "I don't know, Colonel."

"Just before you landed at Dhahran," Hemingway began, "I reported to Washington the South Yemen flight was—"

"Colonel Hemingway!" Kevin Norlin cut in excitedly. *"The President's on our radio now."*

Riyadh

The thirty-one young Saudis—most of them in Western-style clothes—pressed through the chanting crowd surrounding the compound of the Riyadh television station. Openly gripping khanjars in their waistbands, the young men maintained a protective ring around the tallest of their group. Prince Hamud held his head high to emphasize his advantage. His left arm hung in a sling below a heavily bandaged shoulder, and his eyes blazed in anger at the crowd that jostled his entourage.

The young Saudis with Hamud boldly stared down those in the unruly horde who uttered slurs at the modern dress worn by his group. Reaching the entrance to the inner wall surrounding the television station, they found further progress barred by soldiers in the garb of the national guard.

"Let us through!" demanded Hamud.

A sneering sergeant retorted, "Who are you?"

The royal prince bristled at the insult. He enunciated his words with a waspish bitterness. *"Hamud bin Abdul Aziz Al Saud."*

The sergeant lowered his head in brief penitence. "Your Highness, permit me to summon my commander." He pivoted and hastily shoved his way through the cluster of soldiers behind him.

179

Noticing dried blood on the uniforms of the soldiers, Hamud spoke to the nearest. "Where did you fight the invaders?"

The soldier appeared perplexed by the question. Another soldier answered for him. "We killed the infidels."

"Yes, I can see," smirked Prince Hamud, indicating with his good hand the multiple blood-stained watches and rings worn by most of the guardsmen. "*Where else* did the infidels land?" he asked.

"They didn't land," offered the soldier. "We—"

The sergeant returned and roughly pushed the talkative soldier aside. An officer following the sergeant inquired, "Which of you is Prince Hamud?"

"I am," glared the prince.

"And I am Colonel Habib," haughtily responded the officer, saluting casually. "May I ask your purpose here?"

"I wish to make an announcement on the television."

"That is not possible."

"Why not?" snapped the prince.

"No unauthorized persons are permitted within the station."

"Who gives such orders?"

The colonel hesitated. "It is the Crown Prince."

"Then take me to him!" demanded Hamud. "I will speak with my brother."

Habib avoided the prince's eyes as he countered, "Prince Saleem is not here."

"Where is he?" prodded Hamud.

"I do not know," Habib dully replied. His lie

was obvious. Spinning around, Hamud led his followers through the crowd again. As they neared their cars, the congestion of people became even greater.

Hamud's compatriots who were too severely wounded to walk had remained with the vehicles. Now, they regaled the surrounding throng with the origins of the cargo carried by all of the cars except the white Rolls convertible. Secured by ropes to the hoods and trunks of the cars were inert bodies of Cuban soldiers.

Irene sat nervously in the driver's seat of the Corniche, as it was officially forbidden in Saudi Arabia for a woman to drive. The engine was still running, and her green dress fluttered on the antenna where Hamud had insisted it remain. Her escort in Hamud's absence, Prince Karrim, held court in the backseat. He had been the first to relate the events at King Khalid Airport to the throng . . . in response to a challenge issued from the crowd at Irene's position behind the steering wheel. Karrim was in the midst of his third and expanded version of the early morning fight when he spotted Hamud. Waving his eager listeners away, Karrim called out to his cousin, "What did you say?"

"Nothing," came the sullen reply. "The Crown Prince lets no one in the station."

"Let us go to the Al-Riyadh then," suggested Karrim. "The newspaper will print the truth."

Hamud shook his head. "They would not be open on this day . . . but we can go elsewhere." He walked to the driver's side of his car and motioned Irene to the passenger side for the first time since receiving his wound.

Prince Hamud placed the Rolls-Royce in gear, applied full brakes, and gunned its engine full bore. After the Saudis in front of his car scattered, Hamud abruptly released his brakes. The convertible shot away from its parking spot, and his entourage followed in the same manner.

The White House

Stunned, the President slumped into a chair, shaking his head slowly from side to side. "Those bastards . . . those *goddamned* bastards," he moaned. "How could they commit such an act?"

"Don't blame yourself, sir," Clayton Walters gently intoned.

Allan Steiner raised an eyebrow a moment to study his secretary of state. It hadn't occurred to him that he *should* blame himself for the deaths of the Americans in Riyadh . . . until Walters had suggested it.

"It's a terrible tragedy, sir," Edward Rolle offered. The CIA director pushed his chair away from the conference table and strolled over to the Middle East grid map. The oldest man in the room at seventy-three and of ample girth, he made a grandfatherly appearance. He'd come up through the ranks in *The Company* and had demonstrated a facility for avoiding the overly zealous errors of his politically appointed predecessors. When Rolle returned to the President's side, he spoke in a hushed, tentative tone.

"This *could* help solve the Saudi leadership problem."

Absorbed with his thoughts, Allan Steiner failed

to respond. Comparing the fifty-odd deaths of the Americans in the compounds of Saudi Arabia with the tens of thousands who had finally broken Lyndon Johnson, he found little solace.

"What leadership problem?" asked Clayton Walters curiously.

The CIA director glanced at Walters but returned his attention to the silent, brooding President. "Mr. President?" Rolle said quietly. He repeated himself, a bit more loudly.

Snapped from his doleful reverie, the President searched the faces close by for the person who'd spoken. Rolle leaned over to discreetly inquire, "Sir, may I have a word with you by the map?"

The President nodded skeptically and asked Clayton Walters and General Steel to join them at the wall grid of the Middle East. Masking his disappointment at the invitation to the others, Rolle prefaced his question with a slight smile.

"Mr. President, at what percentile of the labor force does a middle class become threatening to a monarchy?"

Wondering what possible relevance it could have to the current situation, the President indulged the question. "Somewhere," he replied, "between eight and ten percent."

Though Rolle already knew the answer, he made his face register concern. "A recent British survey in *The Economist* stated the Saudi middle class now stands at 8.1 percent."

"What are you getting at?" asked the President. Rolle had paused to let the figure sink in.

"It's quite possible the monarchy in Saudi Arabia," stated Rolle matter-of-factly, "could be overthrown in a time of crisis . . . such as this."

The President turned to his secretary of state: "What do you think, Clayton?"

Walters shrugged. "Inasmuch as the Saud family has consistently taken strong measures to silence any opposition to their rule, I don't know of any instability in Riyadh at this time."

"If it's a stable regime," Rolle smiled, "then why do the Saudis find it necessary to silence their dissenters?"

Walters shook his head. "I don't see the relationship."

"I do," countered Rolle, "and if my assessment of the situation in Riyadh proves accurate, we have a responsibility to encourage a peaceful transition . . . and stable energy sources for our Western allies. On the other hand, if we sit on our hands, Saudi Arabia could easily become another Iran. And that might be little better than Soviet control over the Saudi oil fields . . . *and* reserves."

President Steiner led the three men back to the conference table and sat down. Looking askance at his CIA Director, he spoke in a caustic tone.

"I don't intend to help anyone overthrow the government in Riyadh, Mr. Rolle."

"Of course not, sir," Rolle hastily replied, "but we might encourage a more moderate, enlightened leadership to come forward."

The President rubbed his temple roughly. "Clayton, we need your input."

Walters frowned at Rolle. "I would have to admit that we—the free world for that matter—would benefit by a more enlightened rule in Saudi Arabia, but that doesn't mean we should cause it to happen."

Rolle quickly replied, "I agree with you, Clayton, completely. It would be foolhardy to commit any covert acts in this regard. I might also point out"—Rolle switched his attention to the President—"when our national press gets wind of the number of Americans killed by Saudis, there's going to be hell to pay . . . if you'll pardon the expression, Mr. President."

"And a change in the Saudi leadership," continued the President, "might appear as adequate atonement."

Rolle couldn't immediately tell whether Allan Steiner was being facetious or serious. "I'm not a politician, sir," Rolle too humbly offered.

"Both Saleem and Rahman appear to be involved in the deaths of Americans," stated the President. "Who else could assume the leadership, Mr. Rolle?"

The CIA director shook his head slightly. "I doubt if Prince Rahman had anything to do with the Puller, sir—directly or indirectly."

"Why do you think that?"

"He's ambitious *and* careful, sir. Rahman is next in line behind Saleem for the throne, but by the time Asad dies and Saleem reigns, Rahman may be an old man. Therefore, he would do nothing which might jeopardize a quicker route to the kingship."

"For the sake of discussion," said President Steiner "how would we *encourage* Rahman forward?"

Rolle glanced purposefully at the Middle East

wall grid to delay his reply. "By making him a hero, sir."

"And how do you intend we do that?" asked the President.

"With a little help from General Steel," replied Rolle. "In your press conference, sir, you announced our troops had moved into Dhahran to counter the threat of the Iranian army. Since that army is incapacitated at this time, why not move more Saudis northward and push the Iranians out of Kuwait . . . with Rahman as their field commander?"

"So he returns a hero," agreed the President, "but that doesn't solve the problem of shoving the king and Saleem aside."

"Saleem's disgraced himself," replied Rolle, "and Asad has a heart condition. If Rahman emerged from this crisis in a position of strength, his immediate future would be greatly enhanced."

"I still don't intend to help topple the current regime," reiterated the President.

"We wouldn't have to," Rolle insisted. "Prince Rahman can handle the situation himself, if and when the opportunity arises. And if it does, Saudi Arabia would be replacing a near-maniac and his subservient half-brother king for a man dedicated to bringing his country out of the Middle Ages."

The last statement was an exaggeration, but Allan Steiner chose not to dispute it. He gradually pivoted in his chair to the secretary of state. "Clayton, I won't approve helping Rahman without your concurrence."

Walters stroked his chin. "Mr. President, when I stop to think about the 40,000 Americans still in

Saudi Arabia, I can become exceedingly concerned with the current leaders. I don't particularly like Rahman, but he's better than the alternatives as long as we have no role in what happens to the king and Saleem.''

The President made a wry face. ''General Steel, how would you implement the ouster of the Iranians from Kuwait?''

''The Saudis have 45,000 soldiers on their northern border already,'' replied Steel. Eleven thousand more could be shuttled from their oil fields. If necessary, our F-18s could neutralize the Iranian armor and air power.

Allan Steiner looked to Rolle. ''How do we contact Rahman?''

''He's in Riyadh awaiting our instructions, sir.''

With the vague sense he'd been had, President Steiner spoke with a bitter quality. ''I'd like to speak with Rahman personally before he heads north.''

''He can be at ARAMCO within an hour, sir.'' Rolle picked up a phone and dialed. The men around the conference table listened intently to his subdued words.

''Bring the Lion to Dhahran.''

ARAMCO

Dori ran into the bedroom. "Prince Saleem's on TV again!"

Carrying Hemingway on his board, the men moved into the living room. "Turn up the sound, Dori," requested her father.

"There's something wrong with it, Daddy." As she manipulated the set's controls, they watched the Crown Prince shoving at men who blocked the camera's view of him in the jammed studio of the Riyadh television station. Jostled from behind by other members of his staff, Saleem whirled about and summoned his bodyguards. Tall white-uniformed Bedouins used the stocks of their rifles to wedge their way through the crowd and formed a tight circle around Saleem.

The angry prince grasped the microphone and appeared to be shouting into it. His body noticeably bobbing up-and-down in excitement, Saleem accentuated his words with flailing arms.

Dori giggled. "He looks like a flying chicken."

"What a nerd," exclaimed Kevin.

Even Asad was inwardly amused at the spectacle of his brother making a fool of himself.

The Egyptian station manager squeezed past the circle of bodyguards and flipped the 'on' switch of the microphone—an act which instantly halted Saleem's delivery.

The Crown Prince glowered at the Egyptian and then at the microphone.

"It is on now," meekly explained the station manager.

"You two-legged goat!" exploded Saleem . . . now live on both camera and sound. Calming himself, the Saudi prince started over. His words, translated into English, appeared along the bottom of the TV screen in the ARAMCO living room.

"In the name of Allah, listen to my words. The brave men of my national guard have defeated the invaders at King Khalid airport!" Deafening acclaim at this announcement continued in the small studio until less Saleem motioned for quiet.

"We have killed many infidels," Saleem went on, "yet they injured not one of us. The enemy who survived the wrath of my men have returned to the south. Riyadh is now safe . . . Praise to Allah."

Again, pandemonium erupted. Many clasped Saleem, kissing him on his cheeks and lips. Warmly receiving these embraces for a short time, Saleem again called for silence to resume his delivery.

"However, we are still in great danger. Our king is in the hands of the Americans who have invaded our Eastern Province. My brother, if you are still living, hear my words. We shall find and rescue you! And we shall *drive the infidels from our sacred soil!*"

With these exhortations, the Saudis in the studio repeatedly screamed, "Allah Akbar! Allah Akbar!"

Dori lowered the sound of the TV set.

"He's got to be lying," declared Hemingway. "Potato Joe—one of my Harrier pilots—reported civilian cars on the runways prevented the Yemen flight from landing."

Dori piped up, "Why doesn't someone go over to ARAMCO TV and tell the truth?"

"Honey," gently replied Ambassador Clark, "no one would believe us."

"They *will* believe me," came from the back of the room.

The Americans pivoted as one to face Asad, who repeated, "They will listen to me."

Clark's tone was dubious. "What would you say?"

"What is true," said the king sadly.

The ambassador studied Asad apprehensively. "Let's talk to Washington first." After Clark related the words of the Crown Prince and Asad's offer over the ham radio, President Steiner asked to speak to the Saudi king, who took the chair before the radio.

"Asad, after what's happened in your country," began the President, "your statement could be critical to the future of Saudi Arabia. I think we should discuss what will be said."

"Your suggestions are welcome, Allan."

"First, you must state it was American Marines and planes which compelled the flight from Afghanistan to withdraw." The President paused to ask, "Is someone writing this down?"

"I will," volunteered Clark.

"The next point Asad must mention is crucial. It is the fact that *he* invited our Marines to enter Saudi Arabia. Is that clear, Asad?"

"I understand," replied the king.

"You must also," declared the President with emphasis, "call for the arrest of those responsible for the murder of Americans."

"Mr. President," interjected Clark, "I forgot to reveal earlier that half of the compound's residents in Riyadh were British and French."

"I think it would be helpful," continued the President, "if Asad personally requests his countrymen to safeguard the lives of all Westerners in Saudi Arabia."

"I will say all that you mention," agreed Asad.

There was silence on the ham radio before Allan Steiner resumed speaking in a lowered voice. "Asad, I am greatly bothered by what happened in Riyadh. Why were even the women and children killed?"

The Saudi king hesitated, knowing a non-Arab could never understand. "It is difficult to explain," he offered.

"Try me, Asad. I need an answer . . . for my people."

"It is a custom of the desert," Asad haltingly began. "In war, we either show great compassion . . . or none at all. When peace cannot be made by intermarriage, it is common to show mercy to no one. The women, especially the children, cannot live for they will seek to avenge the men who have died."

"That's crazy!" retorted the President. "Those Americans were not a desert tribe, and they were *not* at war with you!"

The king replied weakly. "Not all Saudi—"

President Steiner cut him off. "Ambassador, did you get everything down on paper?"

"Yes, sir."

"I would like to speak confidentially to you and your Air Force attache now."

Rather than carry the Marine colonel from the room again, Clark asked, "Colonel Hemingway's on the bed beside the radio. Can he remain here?"

"On the bed?"

"Yes, sir. I believe he has a serious back injury."

"Of course, he can stay. Is everyone else out?"

"It's just the three of us, sir."

"Were you able to bring out the tape of Asad's discussion with his brothers in the embassy?"

"We have that, sir. Plus his conversation with you this morning."

"Ambassador, on the way to the television station, I want you to remind the king we have evidence of his complicity in the massacre in Riyadh. And put a copy of the tapes on a plane to Washington immediately."

"Yes, sir."

"I have someone who wishes to speak with Major Fricke now," stated President Steiner.

Clark didn't recognize the voice.

"Major Fricke, are you still a bachelor?" inquired the CIA director.

"Confirmed," replied Fricke, acknowledging the coded question.

Rolle's voice was friendly. "Isn't it about time you *got* married?"

"When I do," Fricke genially responded, "you'll be the first to know."

The President came back on the radio. "Ambassador, Prince Rahman will be joining you soon in ARAMCO. When he arrives, bring him to this radio immediately."

"Yes, sir. May I inquire why he's coming."

The President hesitated. "I can't say over the air yet. After Asad appears on TV, give me a report."

"We'll tape it for you, sir," replied Clark.

As Asad and his Royal Guard officer stepped from the holicopter at ARAMCO TV, Fricke extended both hands to the king. "I'll take the child now, Your Majesty."

Asad continued to cradle the body in his arms. "I must show my people what Prince Saleem's fools have done," he explained.

Fricke looked to Clark, who nodded in assent. The four men walked briskly to the entrance of the television station where they were met by its British manager. Clark told him, "The king wants to make an immediate statement on television. Can you hook up with the stations in Riyadh, Jeddah, Medina, and Damman?"

"If they're willing," replied the Briton.

"Tell them," Asad spoke sternly, "it is *my* will."

In the station studio, Clark gave the king the sheet of paper on which he'd taken notes from President Steiner. Asad looked it over and announced, "It would be best if I did not read from this. I shall remember everything without it."

Before the ambassador could protest, Asad spoke brusquely to the station manager. "I am ready to speak now." The king unwrapped the bundled child and handed the boy to his Royal Guard officer.

His presentation was in marked contrast to the heated harangue of his half-brother. Asad began in a weak voice, so low the control room increased it electronically.

"In the name of Allah, heed my words. My brother, Crown Prince Saleem, who spoke earlier to you, is poorly informed. That I am in the Eastern Province is true, but I am not a prisoner. I came here to direct the defense of our oil fields. And with the help of the Americans whom I invited into the kingdom, the invaders from Afghanistan have been repulsed."

Asad turned to his Royal Guard officer and took the child before continuing. "Do not be alarmed by the blood on my thobe. It is not my own. It comes from the body of this American child . . . and this child comes from a foreign compound in Riyadh where all were killed. Were it not for our American friends, this could be one of my children . . . or one of yours.

"Those who killed the Americans in this compound," Asad continued in a slightly raised voice, "must be brought to justice. A witness observed trucks of the national guard leaving the compound. I call on Prince Saleem to arrest those responsible for this piteous crime. And I call on all Saudi citizens to protect those foreigners who have helped defend our kingdom on this day. Praise to Allah."

With that, Asad waved the camera away and slumped to a nearby sofa.

The White House

"Jim," began the President, "bring the congressmen down again. Don't say anything about the Lockeed compound yet."

Noting a quizzical expression from his secretary of state, Allan Steiner explained, "We've got to prepare an announcement for the press, and I want some political heads to bounce ideas off of."

Arriving in a jubilant mood, the congressmen congratulated the President on the Soviet defeat at Dhahran. After he'd invited them to be seated, Senator Farrell spoke first.

"What's happened to the flight coming up from Yemen?"

"Our latest communication indicates the Saudis managed to prevent its landing also," replied the President without emotion. "We have other news from Riyadh, though, which is why I've asked you to join me. Our ambassador has reported elements of the Saudi national guard massacred a compound of Westerners in the capital."

In the silence which followed, Speaker Snell asked, "How many Americans?"

"Approximately fifty . . . and as many more British and French citizens."

"That's incredible!" exclaimed Farrell. "Why?"

President Steiner briefly looked away from his questioner. "We don't know for certain . . . other than Crown Prince Saleem objected to our Marines entering his country."

"For Christ's sake!" exploded Farrell. "The Marines came in to protect his goddamn country."

"Saleem commands the Saudi national guard," offered Clayton Walters, "which is composed of desert Bedouins. They're noted for their vengefulness and unpredictability."

"That's an understatement." Farrell glared.

"Mr. President, what're we doing to protect other Americans in Saudi Arabia?" asked Snell.

"Marines have been sent into compounds of the Eastern Province, and King Asad is at ARAMCO TV right now, making a statement on our behalf."

"Why don't we seize the Saudi oil fields," suggested Farrell coldly, "to guarantee the safety of Americans?"

"That might endanger our citizens," injected Walters "more than it would safeguard them."

Senator Winslow calmly inquired, "Mr. President, how do you propose to explain the massacre to the American people?"

Allan Steiner eyed Winslow impassively for a moment. "What would you tell them, Senator?"

"It's not what the American people should be told," Speaker Snell broke in. "It's what they'll *accept.*"

Clayton Walters' voice was speculative. "We could announce Arab radicals committed the massacre."

"That's without a doubt!" quipped Snell.

"Mr. President," said Farrell, "if the Saudis had

slaughtered 50 civilians in a Russian compound, I can assure you what would happen. The Russians would come in and line up 500 Arabs!"

Allan Steiner visibly flinched.

"I was only making a comparison," added Farrell, "not suggesting anything."

"Last week," began Winslow, "I read that most of the Saudi foreign monetary reserves are here in the States . . . and they amount to 85 billion dollars. We could confiscate some of those assets as reparations and freeze the rest to guarantee the safety of Westerners in Saudi Arabia."

"Why not *keep* the rest?" suggested Senator Farrell. "Or dole it out to the banks stuck with defaulted loans from Third World nations who were squeezed when the Arabs jacked up their oil prices?"

"That might be difficult to justify," stated the President, actually looking for comments to support Winslow's proposal.

"Not to the American people," retorted Farrell.

Receiving no other opinions, Allan Steiner shifted his attention to the Middle East wall map. In view of the congressmen's earlier statements, he hadn't expected the drastic measures they now suggested. He stood up from the table.

"Gentlemen, thank you again for joining me. I'd prefer you not speak with the press until I've had an opportunity to issue a statement."

As the congressmen left, Walters commented to the President, "That Farrell's a real nut."

"Unfortunately," President Steiner nodded. "He's also a better barometer of the American public than the others."

"Sir," offered Hoolihan, "if you're considering the confiscation of Saudi reserves, I'd suggest a freeze order on their bank accounts immediately . . . before they can be wire-transferred."

The President nodded. "Notify the chairman of the Federal Reserve to do that." As Hoolihan picked up a phone, President Steiner addressed Clayton Walters. "While we're covering their assets here, why don't you contact the British and French embassies? Inform them of the massacre and suggest they take similar action."

When Hoolihan and Walters completed their calls, they joined the President and Edward Rolle before the Middle East wall grid. Walters asked, "Sir, did you intend to discuss the Russian POWs with the congressmen?"

"No, I already knew what they thought."

"They may be right, sir," said Walters. "And if Derevenko's anxious to get them back, we may be able to negotiate concessions."

"Such as?"

"For one, commitments to stop arming the Middle East."

The CIA director grinned broadly. "Come on, Clayton. They break their commitments as soon as it suits them."

"Even a short-term halt in arms shipments," insisted Walters, "would be valuable."

"On the other hand," argued Rolle, "by delaying the return of the prisoners, we could embarrass Derevenko, and that could be a greater deterrent to his future meddling in the Middle East than a piece of pap—"

"Gentlemen," cut in the President, "I'd rather

have Derevenko owe us. What's important now is
the crisis be defused. Plus, I think world opinion
will more favorably consider our actions against the
Saudis if we act magnanimously toward the Soviets. Jim, get Derevenko on the line. Let's see how
interested he is in getting his men back."

After picking up the red phone and making his
request, Hoolihan appeared to be listening intently.
Waiting a minute, President Steiner asked,
"What're you listening to, Jim?"

Hoolihan covered the receiver. "There's quite a
bit of shouting in the background."

"Repeat my request."

"Hello. President Steiner *is waiting* to speak to the
Premier!"

The interpreter's reply was again, "One moment."

When Hoolihan relayed this, the President took
the phone and loudly exclaimed, "This is President
Steiner! I want to speak with Premier Derevenko.
What is the delay?"

After several awkward starts, the interpreter
managed to speak. "Our premier cannot come to
the phone at this time, President Steiner. What
would you like to say to him?"

"Tell him we're holding nearly 150 of his soldiers in Saudi Arabia and wish to make arrangements for their return."

The interpreter, following a lengthy pause, came
back on the line. "How soon will you return
them?"

"In one week. My secretary of state will make
arrangements with your foreign office." When the
President had hung up the phone, he commented,

"That's not the same interpreter with whom I spoke earlier. Clayton, start making inquiries to our people in Moscow. Find out what's happening in the Kremlin."

"I'd imagine Derevenko is in the frying pan right now," offered the CIA director. "I'll have my people work on it, too."

Feeling a singe himself, Allan Steiner wondered if he was out of his own.

As a throng of thousands now milled and chanted before the compound of the Riyadh television station, gray-robed members of the mutawwa (religious police) gradually filled its front ranks.

At precisely the noon hour, the call of the muezzins blared from the loudspeakers of nearby minarets.

"God is great.

I testify that there is no God but one God.

I testify that Mohammed is His Prophet.

Come to prayers.

Come to success.

God is great.

No God but one God."

It was barely discernible over the clamor of the crowd, and when they failed to respond to the midday call to prayer, the mutawwa began beating on their shoulders with bamboo poles . . . ordering them to their knees.

As the crowd slowly began to kneel, a stout member of the mutawwa turned to the Bedouin national guardsmen blocking the inner entrance to the compound. Confronting the youngest of them, he shouted directly into the soldier's face.

"Face Mecca and kneel!"

The confused soldier glanced to his rear, and the mutawwa pointed to the southwest.

"Mecca is *that* way."

Stuttering, the young soldier said, "I cannot—"

"You *dare not* fail to serve Allah!" shrieked the mutawwa, who then passed through the entrance and repeated his call to prayer among the other Bedouins. More gray-thobed mutawwa immediately followed through the entrance.

Coming up behind the young soldier with whom he'd first spoken, the stout mutawwa used his knees to strike the back of the man's legs. As the soldier's own knees buckled, the mutawwa placed his hands on the man's shoulders and forced him to a kneeling position.

The other members of the mutawwa screamed at the standing soldiers, demanding they follow suit. Before the end of the five-minute prayer period, the entire company of national guardsmen within the inner compound was prostrate with the mutawwa. They were also outnumbered by Saudis wearing thobes of the religious police.

As the minarets called an end to the noon prayers, the driver of a black Lincoln limousine behind the throng opened a door of the car and offered his forearm to an elderly, bearded man. Three others wearing the distinctive gray-white thobes of imams also stepped from the limousine.

Whispers ran through the crowd as they recognized the 82-year-old Grand Imam of the Riyadh Mosque. They automatically parted for the passage of Sheik Muhammed ibn Abd Mansur and his three companions, who closely held their gutras to obscure their faces.

The Bedouin guards at the gate to the inner compound moved aside in obeisance as the sheik and his company passed. Seeing the Grand Imam, the mutawwa converged with him at the door of the television building. They pushed aside the soldiers at the door but stepped back when Colonel Habib appeared from within.

"Praise be to Allah," greeted Habib, seeing the thobes of imams.

"Praise be to Allah," Sheik Mansur intoned.

Only now noticing the Grand Imam, Habib sputtered, "Why . . . why are you here?"

"We are here," began the sheik in a raised voice, "to do the will of Allah."

"And what," Habib uneasily asked, "is the will of Allah?"

The deep-set eyes of the Grand Imam turned hostile. "We come to recite the Koran."

The national guard officer hastily calculated the relative risks to his life from denying the senior member of both the Riyadh clergy and judiciary *or* incurring the wrath of the Crown Prince.

"I am honored," Habib generously replied, "to escort you."

Most of the Saudis wearing the gray thobes of the mutawwa followed the sheik and crowded into the studio. When told he could begin, Sheik Mansur peered mournfully into the camera and spoke in a fatigued whine.

"In the Name of Allah, the Compassionate, the Merciful. There is no god but God. Muhammed is the Messenger of God. Praise be to the Lord of the Worlds, Master of the Day of Judgment. Thee do we worship, and Thine aid we entreat. Show us

The way of those on whom Thou hast bestowed Grace, not of those with whom Thou are Wrathful, nor to those who go astray.''

The Grand Imam paused to glance at Colonel Habib beside him. On the other side of the national guard officer were the three who had accompanied the sheik in his limousine.

''There are forces within our kingdom which threaten our sacred way of life. There is *no force* on this earth as great as the power of Allah. To fulfill our sacred duty in following His will, we must seek truth. Beside me now are those who fought bravely for Allah at our airport. *Heed their words*!''

Sheik Mansur beckoned the three in gray-white thobes to the camera. Two of them threw off their shifts, revealing Western clothes beneath.

Recognizing the taller of the two, Habib raised a hand in front of Prince Hamud. The Saudi prince leaned into the face of the national guard officer and spoke his words with menacing sweetness.

''Go fuck a camel.''

Habib's hand was snatched by two gray-thobed men who pinned his arms to his sides. Noting Western clothes under their thobes, Habib asked in alarm, ''Who are you?''

''You shall learn soon enough,'' sneered one of them.

Sheik Mansur stepped aside for Hamud and Prince Karrim.

''Praise be to Allah!'' began Prince Hamud. ''You have heard *lies* from my half-brother, Saleem. He and his cowardly men fled the airport at the first sign of enemy planes! It is through a miracle of Allah and the bravery of Prince Karrim and many others that the invaders were turned back. If it pleases you, I give proof of our presence at King Khalid Airport.''

Lifting a blood-darkened shirt from his shoulder, Hamud ripped the hospital dressing from its place. Fresh blood poured from the jagged wound at the top of his shoulder, reopened by the violence of his movement. With wild eyes, Hamud turned to his cousin. Karrim pulled off his gutra, exposing a reddened row of stitches across his forehead.

''I've been told,'' continued Hamud, ''our king appeared on television and revealed members of the national guard attacked a Western compound in this city. Do you wish the *truth* of this, too?''

Hamud spun around, his eyes searching among the soldiers in the studio. Pointing at the two nearest, he commanded they be brought forward. Gray-thobed Saudis disarmed the soldiers before forcing them before the camera.

''Hold up your arms!'' snapped the prince.

Hamud pointed to their bejeweled hands and forearms, one of which held six watches. ''These hold jewelry and watches *torn* from bodies in the compound of Westerners,'' he loudly proclaimed.

''Arrest them!'' continued Hamud. ''And all others who wear *proof of their guilt!*

The mutawwa, with the help of Hamud's retinue who'd disguised themselves in gray thobes, speedily disarmed the other soldiers in the room and knocked them senseless with bamboo poles. This completed, many of the gray-thobed Saudis rushed from the studio to mete out similar treatment to the guardsmen outside the building.

Hamud stepped away from the camera and went

to the side of Irene who'd accompanied Karrim and him into the building. Removing her headdress, he took her firmly by the wrist and led her to the camera.

"This woman was at King Khalid Airport," began Hamud in a low voice, "when we were attacked. Many cars fought the enemy planes, but it was my car which blocked their final attempt to land."

The Saudi prince lifted her hand high. "This is the *hand* which steered my car at that moment!" He paused before exclaiming, "It is the hand of an American!"

In the ARAMCO compound, the reception of this news was as enthusiastically received as it was by the Saudis in the studio of Riyadh TV.

Louis Fricke placed a hand on the shoulder of the dumbstruck American ambassador. "What was your daughter doing at Riyadh's airport?"

Clark shook his head, keeping his eyes on the television image of Irene among the cheering Saudis. "She's supposed to be on the Riviera with her sister," he finally responded.

"Thank God," Fricke uttered, "she isn't."

The White House

"This call's for you, Ed," said Hoolihan.

The CIA director took the phone. "Rolle here."

"Sir, this is Kamsler. We've isolated the jamming source in the Persian Gulf. It's a Czech-registered freighter that delivered cargo to Kharg Island seventy-two hours ago."

"Where is it now?" Rolle inquired.

"Thirty miles north of Dhahran, just outside Saudi territorial waters."

"Good work, Len." Rolle put the phone down and announced the news.

General Steel responded with uncommon briskness. "We've got to blow that ship out of the water."

President Steiner raised an eyebrow.

"We have the Connie and 15,000 troops from Europe coming into that sector," explained Steel, "and right now, there's no way you or I can effectively control them. All we have is an unsecured, civilian ham radio."

"I'm aware of that, Bob," the President replied, "but I'm not sure we want to *blow* it out of the water."

"Why don't we simply borrow it?" suggested the Marine Commandant. "I, for one, would like to see their technology. Jamming satellite communications is something *we* haven't developed yet.''

"How would you do that?'' Steel asked.

Huering smiled. "It could be done with three Marines.''

The JCS chairman squinted at the commandant. "Three Marines?''

"Three Recon Marines.'' Huering nodded. "Two to foul the props, and a third for the ship's fresh air funnel.''

"Mr. President,'' began Rolle, "I agree with General Huering. I also have an idea how we could get the ship into a friendly port.'' The CIA director explained his plan, which was immediately approved and relayed to Louis Fricke in ARAMCO.

After an hour's further discussion, Allan Steiner arose from the conference table and scanned the faces of his military and civilian advisors. "That's settled. We stay in Saudi Arabia and confiscate their foreign monetary reserves. Jim, raise Ambassador Clark on the radio.''

ARAMCO

Ambassador Clark leaned into the microphone of the ham radio. "We received word ten minutes ago that Prince Rahman landed in his own jet at Dhahran, Mr. President."

"I want you to tell Rahman we have two conditions for helping him," the President stated. He outlined them.

"Rahman may welcome our continued military presence," Clark replied, "but I strongly doubt he'll cooperate if we tell him we're taking their foreign reserves."

Fricke added, "I believe the Ambassador's right, sir."

"Mr. President," Clark began, "it may be prudent to present our conditions as accomplished facts after Rahman returns." *And,* he mused, *after Irene's out of Riyadh.*

"You may be right," President Steiner conceded. "We'll wait."

John Norlin poked his head into the bedroom to report the arrival of Prince Rahman.

"He's here," Clark announced over the radio. "Do you wish to speak to him, sir?"

The President debated a moment. "No, not yet

. . . but I'd like to listen to your discussions with him.''

Rahman entered the bedroom and, after a short exchange, asked to see his brother privately. As Fricke lead Rahman to the bedroom where Asad rested, he hastily described the plan to clear the Iranians from Kuwait.

At the door of Asad's bedroom, Prince Rahman waved the Royal Guard officer outside before entering and closing the door. After awakening Asad, Prince Rahman offered to obtain coffee for the two of them.

At the ham radio, Ambassador Clark asked to speak to the President again. ''Sir, I almost forgot. A young prince of the Saud family appeared on Riyadh TV and confirmed that the national guard was responsible for the Lockheed compound. The same prince led the civilians whose cars stopped the Yemen flight from landing at King Khalid Airport. My oldest daughter, Irene, was with him at the time.''

''*Your daughter?*''

''Yes, sir. Evidently, she helped them.''

''Are you certain of this?''

''That's what the prince said . . . on national television.''

''You should have told me this earlier.''

''I'm sorry, sir. Considering the importance of the other matters we were discussing, it didn't occur to me until now.''

''What's the name of this prince?''

''Hamud, sir.''

''Try to establish contact with him,'' ordered the President.

Rahman, after requesting coffee of the Norlins, insisted on serving the cups himself. Before re-entering the king's bedroom, Rahman briefly visited an adjacent bathroom, where he emptied the contents of eight Sominex capsules into one of the cups.

As the Saudi king sipped the coffee, he shook his head in disgust at the fouled black liquid. Rahman smirked and commented, "Western coffee is hardly fit for a child." He watched his brother closely . . . and reached over to remove the cup from Asad's hand as the king slipped into unconsciousness. After arranging his brother comfortably on the bed again, Rahman rinsed Asad's cup with coffee from his own and threw the residue into a corner of a closet.

When Prince Rahman rejoined the Americans in the bedroom, Fricke explained the proposed invasion of Kuwait in greater detail. "On your return," he concluded to the Saudi prince, "you will be irresistible to your people."

Rahman remained straight-faced. "Can you send your Marines with me?"

Ambassador Clark shook his head. "I am certain the President would not approve the commitment of American soldiers against a Middle East army."

"Besides," Fricke added, "your men have all been protected by the flu vaccine. Ours have not."

Continuing his false show of indecision, Rahman asked, "How can I be assured of success in the north?"

"You will have total air superiority," replied Fricke.

"How can that be?" Rahman asked sourly. "I no longer have an air force."

"The Constellation is moving into the Gulf," revealed Fricke.

Rahman blinked in surprise.

"She's taking up a battle station on the other side of Qatar," continued Fricke, "and tonight we'll drop leaflets over Kuwait warning of a full-scale attack tomorrow by a joint Saudi-Iraqi force."

"I must have more than paper," Rahman muttered.

"You will," responded Fricke. "Our F-18s will provide air cover. The Saudi insignia is being painted over ours. They will be fully capable of providing any assistance you require, and I shall personally accompany you."

"Then let us begin." Rahman smiled for the first time. "We must act quickly before the effects of the flu wear off. I will say goodbye to my brother and we shall leave."

After checking Asad's pulse, Prince Rahman rushed back to the Americans. "Ambassador Clark, you must help me," pleaded Rahman. "The king is ill!"

"What's wrong with him?" asked Clark in equal alarm.

"I cannot wake him!" replied Rahman, casting a furtive glance at Fricke and adding, "It may be another heart attack."

"We'll get him to the ARAMCO hospital immediately," said Clark.

Rahman shook his head. "No, the king must see his British specialists."

"Where are they?" asked Clark.

"London," answered Rahman with a hopeful note.

Clark looked at the Saudi prince in consternation. "You want us to take Asad to London?"

"No," replied Rahman. "The royal hospital plane will do that."

"Ambassador," interjected Fricke, "they have a 707 with a fully equipped emergency room for heart attack victims. I believe that's what Prince Rahman is speaking of."

"Well, where is it?" asked Clark in some confusion.

"It should be arriving at Dhahran in a short while," Rahman announced. "I took the precaution of ordering it to follow me."

"Precaution?" repeated Clark, looking to Fricke for more explanation. Fricke shrugged his shoulders.

"Yes," nodded Rahman. "It normally follows the king whenever he travels. It carries three doctors, including a cardiologist."

"We'll get Asad to the ARAMCO hospital for now," decided Clark, "and transfer him to his plane later." As they started to leave the bedroom, Hemingway broke his silence.

"Major Fricke, I've got a suggestion for that leaflet you're planning to drop over Kuwait." While the others carried the Saudi king to a helicopter, Hemingway described his idea to Fricke.

Later, after Clark had concluded his report to Washington, the President asked, "How did Colonel Hemingway injure his back?"

"I've been told," replied Clark, "that he was forced to crashland in the process of stopping two truckloads of marauding Saudi national guardsmen. Half his face is burnt to a crisp, too. And he's refused to go to the hospital."

"Colonel Hemingway," the President called out. "Can you hear me?"

"Yes, sir," the Marine replied.

Allan Steiner selected his words with care. "Is the situation well in hand, Colonel?"

"Yes, sir," Hemingway repeated. "I've turned over my command to Colonel Caliguiri who came in from the Med."

"Then it's my wish," stated President Steiner firmly, "that you proceed immediately to the hospital, Colonel."

When the Marine officer didn't respond, Clark did. "I'll arrange transportation at once, Mr. President."

The White House

Slamming his empty coffee cup on the conference table, General Huering nearly bowled over his chair in getting up. He hurried to General Steel's side.

"Bob, why haven't we involved the British assault carrier in the northern Gulf?"

The JCS Chairman clenched his eyes at the oversight. They both approached President Steiner in conference with Clayton Walters and Jim Hoolihan.

"Mr. President," interrupted Steel, "the Commandant just reminded me the British have a small carrier in the Persian Gulf . . . which could be decisive in the Kuwait operation."

Huering added, "It's similar to the Puller in capability."

"If the British are invited in," Clayton Walters cautiously offered, "they'll almost certainly ask for a political voice."

Allan Steiner looked directly at his secretary of state. "What's wrong with that? We're going to have a difficult enough time justifying our actions in Saudi Arabia, much less in Kuwait, too. Jim, get Prime Minister Colburn on the line."

"Mr. President," said Rolle, "assuming the Iranians are driven out of Kuwait, do we want the Saudis to retain a military presence there?''

"No, of course not.''

"The British would solve that problem for us,'' continued Rolle.

"I have Colburn, sir,'' announced Hoolihan, as he switched on the table speaker and handed over the phone.

"Chet, this is Allan. How are you?''

"Very good, Allan. What's going on? We've frozen Saudi assets as Clayton Walters suggested.''

After describing the aborted invasions and the Kuwait plan to his British counterpart, President Steiner said, "I've called to suggest your carrier in the Gulf assist in the Kuwait operation.''

"Why don't your own forces handle the job?''

"A Saudi gunboat torpedoed our assault carrier.''

"A Saudi gunboat?'' queried Colburn. "How'd that happen?''

"We don't know yet, Chet. We don't know why they killed everyone in the Riyadh compound either.''

"What do you intend to do about it?''

"We're still discussing the matter. Our main concern now is eliminating the Iranian threat.''

"I see,'' Colburn broadly replied, deciding to prod for additional information. "Are you positive the Saudis require our assistance.''

"We're uncertain of Rahman's ability to confront the Iranians, however debilitated they may be.'' Sensing Colburn's reserve, the President posed his own question. "Do you think we should also ask the French to participate?''

"No," answered Colburn instantly. "I don't think that's quite necessary. The French can be difficult to deal with."

"Fine," concluded Allan Steiner. "Have your navy coordinate with Admiral Sparks on the Constellation. It's steaming into the Gulf right now."

"I'm not certain we can reach our people in the Gulf," replied Colburn. "Our communication has been out."

"Damn," muttered President Steiner, having forgotten his own communications problem.

Ed Rolle extended his hand to get the President's attention. "Can the British still communicate with their ambassador in Oman?"

The President nodded. "Chet, if you can get a message to Oman, we can fly it into your carrier."

"I suppose my people could do the same," replied Colburn. "We have ships south of Oman with whom we've been talking."

"That's settled then. For the time being, Chet, I'd like to see your military remain in Kuwait. We'll encourage the Saudis to leave as soon as possible."

"That should pose no problem. The Kuwait government invited us into their country during a similar crisis in 1961. I'm sure they would much prefer us over the Saudis."

Rolle placed a hand-written note before the President.

"Chet, your military people must be inoculated against the influenza. The necessary vaccine can be delivered to your consulate in Bahrain within the hour."

"This is all quite irregular, Allan. I suppose

we've little choice, though. Kuwait holds a tenth of the world's oil reserves.'' Colburn paused for the American leader's response.

"Their oil's a powder keg . . . just like the Saudi oil, Chet. With you sitting on it, I'll be much relieved.''

"Are you going to be *sitting* to the south, Allan?''

After a short pause, the President replied, "As long as there's a threat.''

"That could be quite some time, Allan.''

"That's what we've been thinking.''

In the Persian Gulf

The two Gulf Oil supertankers, moving sluggishly through the night water, passed one-half mile east of the anchored Czechoslovakian-registered freighter. Further to the east and screened by the tankers, an American submarine quietly surfaced and dispatched a rubber raft with three men. In their black wetsuits and hoods, the Marines blended well with the murky surface of the oil-slicked waters. As their sub slipped under the waves again, the men adjusted the water cylinders in their inflated raft. By the time the swells of the first tanker reached them, the raft had disappeared just below the surface.

"Line up!" ordered Lieutenant Hardie. The two other men positioned their hand-held waterfans on either side of the officer's fan.

"All right," Hardie announced, "move out!" Each of the fans was attached to the barely-submerged raft which now trailed behind the men.

The aft lookout on the freighter lit another cigarette with the smoldering butt of his first one and then flicked the butt into the water thirty feet below. He watched the red glow hit the water, taking little notice of the passing supertankers now turning sharply eastward, away from his ship.

The bow of the freighter was more active. Katrina, a tall, thick-thighed Ukrainian in her late thirties, checked the deck behind her to see if it was clear. That she was still ummarried was better explained by the bulk of her figure than its six-foot-two height. Her dark brown hair was worn long to better frame her two strongest assets, one of which was a moderately attractive face. The other asset occasionally interfered with the pleasure she sought at the bow of the ship.

"Frederic," she whispered.

An equally cautious voice called out, "Over here."

Watching her feet, Katrina stepped through piles of coiled ropes and moved toward the voice. A hand reached out to clutch the woman's broad skirt and roughly pulled her off-balance. Landing hard among the ropes, she coarsely mumbled, "*You pig!*"

"Yes, my pudding," Frederic agreed. "I am a hungry pig!"

Grabbing her loose blouse, he yanked it up. As she struggled to pull it the rest of the way over her head, he clutched a mountainous breast in his hands and feverishly buried his face in its warmth.

"Stop that, you fool!" protested Katrina, shaking her chest and jerking away. "I am not a *cow.*"

Frederic, a full foot shorter and considerably lighter than his lover, reconsidered his approach. Gazing at her full bosom in the moonlight, he placed his fingertips just below her shoulders and followed the flow of soft skin down to the rounded peaks of the breasts—each one larger than his head.

"My dear," he soothed, "you are a poor man's Sophia Loren."

Katrina snickered. "Compared to me, she is but a child."

Frederic kissed the tips of her other asset.

"Come, little man," she beckoned. "Tonight, it is your turn first."

She knew Frederic would not last long above, for he had little stamina. And there was no place he could comfortably prop his arms . . . as her shoulders were too wide, and the flesh of her immense bust overflowed into the space between her ribs and arms when she reclined on her back.

Three hundred yards from the freighter, Lieutenant Hardie split off from the two other Marines, who slipped on aqualungs before continuing with the raft.

When the lieutenant reached the bow, he attached a bearclaw (magnetic clamp-ring) as high as he could reach on the ship's side. After tying his fins and waterfan to the bearclaw, he pulled half his body out of the water and attached himself to its ring with a loop from his belt. From a watertight packet on his chest, he removed an arc-gun and four electronic suction cups, two of which he fitted onto his knees and the others to his hands. Buttons controlled by his thumbs and toes could release the suction of the cups.

Fifty yards from the stern, the two other Marines adjusted the raft to drop another ten feet below the surface before pulling it to the side of the freighter and securing it to the hull with a bearclaw. Removing tools and a coil of cable from the raft, they made their way down to the twin screws of the ship.

At the other end of the freighter, Hardie slowed his ascent as he approached the opening in the bow for the anchor chain. He poked his head into the opening and saw something move. Instantly dropping down, the Marine officer pulled his arc-gun from its holster and waited for the lookout to peer over the railing of the ship.

In the stillness, Hardie thought he heard the faint slapping of waves on the sides of the ship. Interspersed with these sounds, he also noticed deep animal-like noises coming from above. When the rhythmic grunting did not come nearer, the lieutenant inched his head above the rim of the anchor opening again.

Fifteen feet away, the moonlight illuminated what appeared to be a pair of great white balloons pumping up and down like giant pistons. Confused by the sight, Hardie wiped the salt water from his eyes and looked again. It was several seconds before he distinguished among the ropes a smaller second body under the heaving buttocks of the first one. Realizing what he was witnessing, Hardie stared a moment longer and dropped out of sight. *My gawd,* he grinned, *that gal's gonna pump a gusher.* He debated whether to wait or not. Having duly considered the question, the lieutenant raised himself and aimed his weapon.

A dark blue arc appeared for an instant between the muzzle of the weapon and Katrina's right buttock. The charge caused her to stiffen and jerk upright. She swayed unevenly.

"Katrina . . . oh, Katrina," moaned Frederic in ecstasy.

Hardie couldn't stifle a short chuckle before pulling his trigger again.

The woman's body shuddered and started to topple forward. Feeling part of the last charge himself, Frederic tried to twist away from the falling body. Katrina fell solidly over her lover.

Hardie hastily pulled himself over the railing, shifted his suction cups aside, and crawled to the struggling, semi-buried man.

"Sorry, Romeo," offered Hardie. He touched the arm of the trapped Russian with the muzzle of the arc-gun and squeezed again. Frederic quivered . . . then lay as still as the woman atop him. The lieutenant craned his neck down to locate the man's head. Not finding it, he checked the other side of the woman. Seeing nothing there either, he nudged Katrina's body sideways and located the man's face. Confirming he was also unconscious, Hardie let the woman's body settle over her lover again.

The American paused to check in the direction of the ship's bridge. Smiling to himself, he gathered the clothes of the couple and flung them overboard before moving away in a crouch.

Twenty feet from the couple, he stopped and quickly retraced his steps. Hardie found the lovers and lifted Katrina's right breast with one hand . . . searching for the man's head with his other hand. He grasped Frederic's hair and tugged at the head. When the man was in a position where he again could breathe, the American gently lowered the breast to the side of his face.

The funnel intake for the ship's fresh air was on the bow, as expected. Hardie easily identified it by feeling its inflow of air. Attaching a length of cord to the pins of two gas canisters, he securely taped the containers inside the funnel. After moving a safe distance away, Hardie pulled the cords and heard the hiss of escaping gas.

His descent from the bow was accomplished at twice the speed of his ascent. Recovering his gear, Hardie swam along the starboard waterline of the freighter until he met the other two Marines at midship. They silently moved away from the freighter, keeping the raft underwater until they'd traversed 150 yards.

At that distance, the officer removed a flasher from his chest packet and—shielding it with his head from the freighter—flickered its red beacon twice.

Within seconds, he saw a responding double-flash, and the three men commenced moving further from the ship.

Several minutes later, the rear lookout on the freighter spotted the two Gulf Oil supertankers again. Nine hundred yards directly behind his ship, they were moving at seven knots and precisely side-by-side with an interval of seventy-five yards. When their distance from the freighter had closed to 500 yards, the tankers had slowed to three knots. The lookout, deciding it was too late for the tankers to veer away, notified his bridge.

The commands from the bridge to the engine room went unheeded. Had they been acted upon, the result would have been the same. The ship's screws were hopelessly fouled.

The aft lookout failed to see the double line of anchor chain stretched between the sterns of the supertankers. The weight of the chains kept them well below the surface until the Gulf Oil ships approached on opposite sides of the freighter's stern.

At that point, the chains were winched up until they hung between the supertankers . . . just above the surface.

When the American ships passed the position where the freighter had been, a Saudi fisherman near the shore remarked to his partner, "Where did the little ship go?"

The other fisherman peered out over the moonlit water. "Big fish eat little fish," he lamely offered. "Maybe big ships eat little ships."

Throwing a handful of octupus bait at his half-witted partner, the first fisherman cried out, "You son of a camel turd."

By dawn most of the military equipment aboard the freighter had been removed, its entire hull had been repainted, and the name on its bow had been sandblasted and replaced with a new one.

In the drydock of the Saudi Arabian port of Qatif, a weary group of British shipfitters trudged down the freighter's gangplank.

"Hey, Harve!" yelled a man behind him. "What happened to your shirt?"

The other men sniggered. The story of the embracing lovers at the ship's bow had passed quickly among the workers.

Adjusting the sandblaster on his shoulders, the bare-chested Briton replied, "I gave it to a lady."

"A *ladee*—, you say?" bellowed his taunter. "What's a lady doing stark-naked atop a bloke half her size?"

"Maybe she warn't no lady, mate," recanted Harve, "but I'm still a gentleman."

His laughing friends nearly shoved him off the gangplank.

ARAMCO

Their presence no longer being required at the Saudi/Kuwait border, Prince Rahman and Louis Fricke returned to Dhahran by mid-morning of the next day. As the Saudi prince described his "triumph" in the Norlin living room, Fricke briefed the White House over the ham radio.

"We fired leaflets at them, Mr. President," explained Fricke.

"The Iranians fled because of a *leaflet?*" asked the President incredulously. "What'd it say?"

"It wasn't what it said as much as what it pictured. Most of the leaflet was a blow-up of a photograph taken of an atrocity committed by Saudi soldiers on the Russians at Dhahran."

"I remember Colonel Hemingway mentioning that."

"We doctored the photo a bit," confided Fricke, "so the Russians appeared to be Iranian soldiers."

"Was there any opposition at all?"

"No, sir. The leaflets were dropped late yesterday. By this morning when the Saudi and British units moved in, the only Iranians left were those too sick to move. Almost every car and truck in Kuwait was expropriated by the Iranian army last night."

"How many men did they leave behind?"

"Almost four thousand, sir. Most of whom we transferred onto ships and sent back to Iran."

"I didn't expect such a rapid resolution."

"Wait until you see the leaflet, sir."

"I think I'll pass on that," remarked the President. "Send Rahman in now."

The Saudi prince strode pretentiously into the bedroom and was motioned to sit on the chair near the ham radio by Ambassador Clark, who spoke into the mike. "Mr. President, this is Emory Clark. Prince Rahman and I are both here now."

"Prince Rahman," greeted the President, "I'm pleased your army was able to drive the Iranians from Kuwait so quickly."

Rahman replied in a grave tone "It was the will of Allah."

It was the lack of will of the Iranians, Allan Steiner thought, who paused a long moment and spoke in an even graver tone. "I have a matter I'd like to discuss with you, Rahman. What your people have done at the Lockheed compound in Riyadh is of extreme consequence."

The Saudi prince lowered his voice. "It is to be regretted."

"Is that all you can say?" the President demanded.

Rahman's eyes narrowed and he made no reply.

"You don't even want to offer an apology?" President Steiner scolded, his voice rising.

Rahman nervously glanced at Fricke and saw no support. The CIA man kept his eyes intently on the ham radio.

"Answer me!" Allan Steiner demanded.

Rahman was nearly inaudible. "It is an unfortunate—"

"*Unfortunate*, you say!" exploded the President. "Your people have murdered more than 50 citizens of the United States, and you call it unfortunate!"

A desperate silence pervaded the bedroom.

"I shall see," said Rahman softly, "that those responsible are punished."

Allan Steiner stated, "I understand that includes the king, Saleem, and yourself. What punishment do you have in mind?"

Rahman replied, "I cannot be held responsible for the acts of those who follow Prince Saleem. The men under my command have not harmed Americans."

"Who ordered the attack on the Puller?" the President asked abruptly.

"I do not believe the gunboat was Saudi," Rahman nervously offered.

"It flew your flag."

"Anyone could do that. Iranians . . . South Yemenis . . . even the Russians."

Partially conceding the point, President Steiner continued, "A videotape of the meeting you had with your brothers yesterday at the American embassy has already been delivered to the White House. We know what you told them."

Rahman flashed his eyes at Clark, trying to recall what he'd said with his brothers.

"Where's your brother, Saleem?" the President asked.

"I do not know. My *half-brother* committed a terrible error."

"You are not without guilt yourself, Rahman."

Beginning to grasp the American's intent, the Saudi prince asked his own question. "What is it you want?"

"Rational co-action." The words were spoken with great care.

After a moment, Rahman said; "I do not understand."

Allan Steiner paced his words in short phrases as if addressing a large rally. "To prevent aggression in the future against your country, we believe it would be prudent for Saudi Arabia to reestablish the partnership you had with the American oil companies who originally formed ARAMCO. Such an arrangement would permit us to safely remove most of our military units from your country."

After a significant pause, the President asked, "Do you understand me now?"

By remaining silent, the Saudi prince signified his rebuff of the American's proposal. Each man waited for his opponent to speak . . . and thereby concede. Having played the game longer, President Steiner closed his eyes and patiently began to count. After a full minute, Rahman could hear himself breathe in the stone quiet of the bedroom where every eye seemed to bore into him. When he could stand it no longer, the prince coughed, and started to speak.

"I understand, but—"

"There's more," interrupted President Steiner. "After adequate reparations are made to the families of Westerners slain in your country, we believe the balance of your foreign monetary assets should be utilized to transfer the nonperforming loans of Third World nations to the Saudi national bank."

Rahman's voice became unsteady. "What you ask is—"

"I *ask* nothing!" Allan Steiner asserted. "We're telling you what is going to happen. It was the foolishness of your leaders which left your oil fields open to foreign seizure . . . *and* your greed that indirectly led to the necessity for those Third World loans. The loans are *yours* now."

"I cannot explain this to my people," the Saudi prince whined.

The President turned friendly. "Rahman, as a precaution, the ARAMCO hospital pumped your brother's stomach. We asked them not to tell Asad what they found." He added, "It's fortunate for you that it was *our* doctors who discovered this rather than those on your 707."

The Saudi prince sat motionless before the radio, slowly comprehending how thoroughly he'd been tricked.

"Mr. President," interjected Clark, "I think it would be prudent to also disband the Saudi national guard."

Knowing that this of all the American demands was the most impossible, Rahman quickly protested. "That cannot be done! *They* would not permit it. These men are the direct descendents of the Bedouins who established Saudi Arabia."

"Yes," agreed Allan Steiner, "and later they nearly destroyed your new nation during the Ikhwan revolt. Have you forgotten why your father chose the palm tree of the settled, rather than the camel of the wandering Bedouin, for your national flag?"

Rahman was taken aback by the American's knowledge.

The former history professor answered his own question.

"Because the Bedouin could not be trusted, Rahman. They fought for whoever offered the most money or bounty . . . and to this day they have not changed. You must rid your country of this scourge."

"I do not dispute your words," replied Rahman, "but to disband the Bedouins would only make them more uncontrollable. It would be better to spread them among my land forces."

Clark glanced to Louis Fricke who nodded in agreement. The Ambassador leaned over the mike. "Mr. President, I would concur with Rahman's suggestion."

"Tomorrow," concluded President Steiner, "we will both hold press conferences to announce these actions."

Rahman muttered, "I will have difficulty explaining this to my family."

"It will not be as difficult as the explanation I must give my people," countered the President; "for what your national guard has done."

When the prince made no further response, Allan Steiner told him, "Rahman, you were lucky this time. Tell that to your family."

"Tom, why'd you wait so long to come here?"

Still doped by the drugs they'd given him prior to surgery the previous night, Tom Hemingway repeated Sandi's question to himself, trying to get it clearer in his mind. When he'd awakened, she had been there—sleeping in a chair, her head and arms resting on his bed. He'd gazed at her dark brown hair for some time before realizing who she was. Through the eye holes of his head bandages, he studied her plaintive expression and shook his head slightly.

"I couldn't come earlier."

When she accepted the reply, he was relieved. He didn't want to talk . . . to think anymore. Tom turned away from her eyes and, after a long silence, asked, "Were you there?"

"Where?"

"Last night," he said, "when they worked me over."

"Yes."

He turned further away, again visualizing the hideousness he'd seen in the mirror at the Norlin home.

"I want to rest," sighed Tom.

Sandi stood slowly, understanding the despondency which affected nearly all patients with facial burns. ''I'll tell the doctors you're awake,'' she told him. At the door Sandi hesitated and looked back to see whether his eyes had followed her. They hadn't. Walking silently back to the bed, she gently placed a hand on his arm and spoke softly, ''I love you, Tom.''

It was the first time she'd said the words to him, but he made no reply. Sandi hadn't expected a response, or needed one before she left. The need was his.

A few minutes later, a surgeon entered the room and cheerfully inquired, ''How's the warrior this morning?''

Hemingway paused to contemplate the intruder. ''Not so hot,'' he uttered.

''You're lucky not to be sore at the other end, too,'' smiled the surgeon. ''In cases like yours, we normally carve a piece off the buttock.''

The Marine colonel squeezed his buns together and sensed no pain. He gave the doctor a sideways glance.

Having piqued his patient's interest, the surgeon continued. ''We usually transplant skin from the buttock to replace facial skin. But with your back injury, we decided to give you a break.'' The talkative doctor grinned broadly.

''Where'd you get it?'' asked his patient.

''It's coming from Texas.''

''Texas?'' repeated Hemingway.

''That's right, Colonel. Last night, we put a square-inch of your facial skin on an F-18 to Houston. In five days, we'll get back a square foot.''

''Of what?''

"Skin—an expanded autograft of your tissue culture," explained the doctor. "You'll probably look better after we've finished than you did before dodging that missile."

Hemingway settled easier in his bed. "Thanks, Doc."

"Don't thank me," said the doctor. "Thank the California pathologist who developed the expanded autograft."

"Who was he?"

"As I recall, it was A-something Freeman. Aaron Freeman, I believe."

Hemingway was reminded of the Saudi king. "How's Asad?"

The doctor shrugged. "He was fine when he left here. Except for an elevated blood pressure, Asad was in perfect health. He had no reason to go to London."

Sandi, carrying a tray of food, entered the room.

Winking at the nurse, the doctor addressed the Marine. "Do you know this lady, Colonel?"

The Marine nodded. "We've met."

"Well, I've got a few other patients this morning," said the doctor. "I'll check back later."

"Doc," Hemingway called out, "what's the word on my back?"

"X-rays were negative. Probably just a bad sprain." He waved and left. Without speaking, Sandi set the tray on the bed and began cutting the food into bite-sized pieces. After he'd begun to eat, she commented, "You're scheduled for a sponge bath after breakfast."

He continued chewing his food.

After a short while, Sandi half-smiled without looking up. "Would you like me to give it to you?"

Tom noticed she'd put on new lipstick and brushed her hair since she'd left. He swallowed and waited for the next bite.

"Suit yourself ," Sandi remarked, a twinkle in her eyes. "The other nurse on duty in this wing is Pakistani. When you're finished eating, I'll send *him* in."

The initial alarm in the Marine's eyes was replaced by a brazen stare. "*You* can have the honors," he smiled.

King Khalid International Airport
Riyadh

Prince Rahman was reminded of the scenes he'd viewed as a child. Instead of Saudi horsemen racing across the desert astride their sleek Arabians though, his countrymen swept back-and-forth on the runways below in swift cars. His *victory* had been heralded on every radio and television station in the kingdom, and now it appeared every Saudi male with a vehicle had come to King Khalid Airport to greet the "Liberator of Kuwait."

Each time Rahman made an approach in his F-15, hundreds of cars wildly converged in his landing pattern. Circling the airport after his sixth aborted approach, the fuel warning light on his console flashed red.

The Saudi prince pointed his fighter in the direction of the open desert and reached above his head to grasp the yellow handle attached to the seat. A sharp report followed his downward yank.

Choked with fear, Rahman rode his seat up the rails. Then everything became quiet. As he tumbled backward through space, the seat sailed away from him and Rahman glimpsed parachute lines racing past his head. A moment later, he felt a stiff jolt and his body whipped around. A full canopy blossomed above.

237

Able to breathe again, he gaped at the runways below. From every corner of the airfield, drivers scrambled toward the point where they expected him to land. Rahman was more concerned with avoiding the cars than the shock of hitting the tarmac. The closer he came to the ground, the more deafening was the blaring of the horns. His flight boots made contact with the hood of a Jaguar sedan and slipped beneath him, throwing Rahman's full weight onto the hood.

Before nightfall, the Jaguar owner would be offered three million riyals for his sedan . . . due to the near-perfect outline of Rahman's body on its hood. The owner took particular pride in pointing out the round indentation where the royal prince's helmet had slammed into the metal. Firmly refusing all offers, the car's driver repeated to all who would listen how his car had broken Rahman's fall from the sky.

As the Saudi prince regained consciousness, he found himself being carried above the clamoring crowd by countless hands. This directionless parade continued until the men below finally heard his shouted demands to be put down. Once on his feet, Rahman removed his helmet, unhooked his parachute harness, and began making his way from the center of hundreds of hopelessly jammed cars.

Standing on the front seat of his white convertible, Prince Hamud viewed Rahman's procession slowly winding its way out of the massed cars and people. Hamud directed Irene to drive the Corniche close to the point where Rahman would eventually emerge. The other young men who had become national heroes with Hamud the previous

day had also held back from the tangled charge to
greet Rahman. Their vehicles followed alongside
the Corniche in a column led by Prince Karrim's
new BMW, and a file of jeeps containing members
of the Royal Guard flanked Hamud's other side.

Prince Hamud yelled sharply to a Royal Guard
officer in the lead jeep. The officer led a group of
his men into the crowd's perimeter where they
quickly extracted Prince Rahman from his admir-
ers and led him to Hamud.

The two half-brothers embraced emotionally and
sat on the convertible's back seat as Irene twirled
the car away from the encroaching people. The
twenty-eight miles of freeway into Riyadh were
lined with more ecstatic Saudis who'd been unable
to crowd into the airport. After winding through
the capital, the procession ended at Rahman's palace.

Two hours before sundown, the governing body
of the country was ushered into the receiving hall
of Rahman's royal residence. The eleven eldest living sons of Abdul Aziz Al Saud entered the great
hall in hushed silence, and some were shocked to
see those already seated in the plush, rust-red arm-
chairs along the perimeter of the barren, green
room.

At the center of the high wall opposite the main
entryway sat Prince Rahman, his chair slightly
apart from those on either side. To his left the chairs
were empty. On his right sat Hamud, Irene, Karrim, and the thirty-one other young men who'd
survived the MiGs and Cubans at King Khalid Airport. All those seated wore the traditional thobe and

headdress, except for Irene, whose chador included a modest veil.

The eldest of Rahman's half-brothers, Prince Benhar, halted in the middle of the hall and waved an arm toward the seated young men whose thobes did not display gold braid. "Who are the non-blooded," he shrilly demanded, "who sit in my presence?"

Prince Rahman turned with casual aplomb to his right. "Of the men who faced the invaders of Riyadh," he boldly retorted, "these are the ones *whose blood still flows.*"

Benhar, unsatisfied with the explanation for the break in protocol, remained fixed in the center of the hall. When the rest of the Royal Council took chairs to Rahman's left, Hamud rose and approached Prince Benhar. Standing but a foot away from the elderly man, he exclaimed in a loud voice, "And *where* were you yesterday, my brave brother?"

Inflamed by the insinuation, Benhar reached inside his thobe and made a show of gripping his khanjar.

A high-pitched voice pierced the thickened atmosphere of the hall. "In the Name of Allah," intoned the Grand Imam of Riyadh, "we are honored in the presence of the warriors for Islam . . . whether they be sitting or standing."

Sheik Mansur, his entrance unnoticed till now, walked unhurriedly to the center of the hall, followed by several senior members of the Ulema. Bowing slightly to the seated young men, the Grand Imam prayed in a lowered voice.

"May Allah bring the warriors of Islam the same

blessings which they have brought to this kingdom.''

The Grand Imam shuffled toward Prince Rahman, taking the first chair to his left. All in the hall had found seats, except for Prince Benhar who made one last effort to save face. ''The infidel woman,'' he spit out, ''must *leave* before I sit!''

''Very well, my brother,'' Rahman smiled back. ''You may remain standing . . . if you wish.''

Doubly insulted, the old prince stalked from the hall.

''Bring in Habib!'' Rahman promptly commanded.

At the same entrance from which the Grand Imam had emerged, two members of the mutawwa escorted Colonel Habib into the hall. One of them pulled the sleeve of the national guard officer; guiding him before the Royal Council. Those in the great room recognized Habib's gait and stiffened back as that of a man suffering the severe welts of the Syrian flail.

The second mutawwa carried a heavily laden basket. When the trio halted, he spewed the contents of the basket before the feet of Habib.

Rings, necklaces, bracelets, watches, and other jewelry clattered angrily across the marble floor. The eyes of the ruling princes fixated on the sparkling array of silver and gold.

''*Colonel Habib!*'' Rahman's voice boomed. ''Who are the owners of the treasure at your feet?''

The officer mumbled his reply with bowed head. ''It belongs to the foreigners of the Lockheed compound.''

"Then *why* is this jewelry in my palace?" thundered Rahman in mock anger.

Habib slumped further. "Because it was taken from the foreigners."

Prince Rahman spoke in a half-whisper. *"Who* took it from the foreigners?"

"Members of the national guard," Habib slowly answered.

"Colonel Habib!" Rahman snapped. "Why were your men in the compound of the foreigners?"

Habib continued his well-rehearsed recitation. "We were in trucks on the way to the airport. As we passed the compound, we were ordered to stop and enter it."

"And *who* gave such an order?" demanded Rahman.

Habib's reply was barely audible. "Prince Saleem."

"In the Name of Allah!" shrieked Rahman. "Does this man lie?"

The mutawwa holding Habib's shirt sleeve loudly replied, "We have the same from three other officers. This one does not lie."

Rahman feigned genuine curiosity. "What were your men to do in the Westerner's compound, Colonel Habib?"

The national guard officer raised his head off his chest. "We were told to beat the foreigners. With our rifles, we struck the men, but when we also hit the women and children, their men protested and tried to seize our weapons. A shot was fired, and then more rifles were fired. In the end, it was necessary to kill everyone . . . that there be no survivors.''

Prince Rahman delivered his last question after a lengthy pause and without anger. ''And who gave this final order?''

' Absolute silence in the hall amplified the dogged voice of the national guard officer. ''I received this order from my commander, Prince Saleem.''

Rahman flicked his wrist, indicating Habib's dismissal.

''Saleem is a madman!'' exclaimed Prince Karrim.

In the spirited discussions which followed, neither Hamud nor Rahman could discern what was being said in the multiple arguments around them. This tumult continued for several minutes until Prince Rahman signalled with a glance to Sheik Mansur. As the Grand Imam stood and paced to the center of the hall, Rahman and Hamud shouted the others into silence.

''In the Name of Allah, the Compassionate, the Merciful,'' began the sheik, ''there can be no doubt who is responsible for bringing shame to our kingdom. And there can be no hesitation for what we must do.''

''We have *no* Crown Prince!'' bellowed Prince Karrim. When the cries of affirmation had subsided, the Grand Imam inquired loudly, ''Where is Prince Saleem now?''

''He boarded the Abdul Aziz,'' replied Rahman promptly, ''in the Red Sea early this morning.''

''So be it,'' announced the Grand Imam. ''The royal yacht shall be his prison. He will not return to the soil of our kingdom.''

Rahman stood on cue. "I shall inform the king."
Sheik Mansur and Rahman left the hall together.

When Asad's hospital room in London was
reached, Rahman described the confession of Colonel Habib and the decision concerning Prince Saleem before handing the phone to the Grand Imam.

For the next hour, Sheik Mansur spoke in hushed
tones with Asad. When he finally placed the phone
in its cradle, the sheik turned to Rahman. "The
king will take full responsibility for inviting the
Americans into the kingdom. He announces his ab-
dication in the morning."

A short while later, after the Grand Imam revealed Asad's decision to those in the palace hall,
the Royal Council reacted as Rahman, Hamud,
and the Grand Imam had anticipated. The new
leaders of Saudi Arabia spent the balance of the
night preparing for the press conference the following morning.

There was little opposition by the ruling council
to the plan they drew up . . . after it was explained
how most of the foreign monetary reserves would
be safeguarded and that production in the oil fields
would be reduced by eighty percent during the
presence of the oil companies.

ARAMCO

"The phone's working!" declared Kevin, startled by its first ring in forty-eight hours.

"Well, answer it," instructed his mother.

Dori jumped up from the breakfast table first and grabbed the phone before her brother. After saying, "Hi," she listened for a moment and looked up. "Mom, a lady wants to talk to Ambassador Clark."

"You'd better wake him up."

Dori ran down the hallway and rapped on the door to Kevin's bedroom.

"Yes?" came a tired voice.

The girl spoke through the door. "There's a woman on the telephone for you."

"I'll be right out," replied Clark. Tucking a loose shirt into his trousers, Emory Clark came into the kitchen and took the phone. "This is Ambassador—"

"Hi, Dad," a cheery voice interrupted.

"Irene . . . where are you?" He quickly added, "Are you okay?"

"Sure, everything's fine," Irene responded. "I'm in Riyadh. At the television station."

"Can you get out of there?" asked her father with great concern.

"Out of where?"

"Riyadh," he pointedly replied.

"Why should I?" Irene blankly asked. "Aren't you coming back?"

"For the time being," he firmly told her, "it's better that you come to Dhahran."

"Dad, we'll talk about that in a minute. I called to tell you who the new king is."

"Prince Rahman," Clark irritably stated, instantly regretting his lapse. Thinking someone might be listening on the line, he asked, "Am I right?"

"Yes," she answered. "How'd you know?"

"I guessed. What's happened to Saleem?"

"He's banned from the country." Irene merrily added, "Guess who the *new* crown prince is?"

"Who?"

"Prince Hamud," she proudly told her father.

"You're kidding?"

"In a few minutes, it'll be announced on Riyadh TV. Hamud asked me to notify you."

"I'm glad you called, honey. And I'm also concerned for your safety. Is there any way you could get to Dhahran?"

"Now?"

"Yes, now."

Irene hesitated. "Dad, after Rahman's coronation tonight, there's going to be a celebration at his palace. I'm invited, and I don't want to miss it."

"*You* were invited?"

"I think I'm part of it. They're going to make me an honorary princess . . . or something like that. I've got to go now, Dad. Watch the TV."

"Honey, be careful."

"Don't worry about me. I've got a thirty-three-man bodyguard."

Clark was puzzled again. "Who are *they?*"

"Hamud and the thirty-two other Saudis who survived the fight at King Khalid Airport."

After a thoughtful pause, Clark told his daughter, "Call me tomorrow, okay?"

"Sure, Dad. Love you."

"I love you, Irene." She had hung up before hearing him. The half-dazed father glanced at the Norlin family gathered around their breakfast table eagerly awaiting some explanation from him.

"That was my daughter," Clark stated vacantly. "She's in Riyadh and acts like she's going to a picnic." He pivoted and started down the hall to his room, then stopped . . . trying to remember something. Spinning around, he exclaimed, "Get everyone up! There's going to be an important announcement on television."

One minute before 5 a.m., the ARAMCO TV station came on the air and revealed they'd be transmitting for Riyadh TV. An imam commenced the recitation of morning prayers. By the end of the prayers, everyone in the Norlin household was gathered close to the TV screen in order to read the English translations.

The face of Sheik Mansur appeared on the screen. When he spoke, his painfully hesitant delivery gave viewers the impression each word had been fastidiously chosen.

"In the Name of Allah, the Compassionate, the Merciful . . . the message I give you is of profound sadness. King Asad has suffered yet another heart attack . . . of greater severity than the ones before.

Due to his condition, he has asked to renounce his throne.''

The sheik continued. ''The Royal Council and the Ulema . . . refusing to accept his decision . . . devoted the hours of last night attempting to dissuade him. Only when the king's physicians pled with us to spare his life . . . did we agree to his renunciation. Saudi Arabia will never have another king . . . who will compare as well to his father— the great Abdul Aziz Al Saud.'' The Grand Imam paused.

''What a crock of—'' Fricke caught himself in mid-sentence. ''I've never heard such baloney.''

''It is my duty,'' the sheik resumed, ''to now reveal the judicial report concerning the conduct of our national guard units at King Khalid Airport two days ago. While Saudi Land Forces fought to the death defending our kingdom, the national guard fled before the infidels arrived. Crown Prince Saleem, their commander, has decided to take full responsibility for the acts of his men. Therefore, he has chosen self-exile . . . and relinquished his succession to the throne of the kingdom. For twelve hours, the Royal Council delayed acceptance of his great sacrifice . . . in the hope he would return to Saudi Arabia. To our sorrow, Prince Saleem has not returned.''

Sheik Mansur stopped to lower his head, as if in prayer.

In the Norlin living room, everyone stirred for the first time in several minutes.

''Yesterday,'' began Fricke, ''Rahman told me he'd been unable to keep his men who survived the initial attack from running also.''

John Norlin asked, "Is *any* of that true?"

"Most of what he said was to save face," explained Clark.

"Whose face?" inquired Norlin.

"Anyone," Clark said, "who's involved with Asad or Saleem."

Sheik Mansur resumed. "When King Asad was told of Saleem's sacrifice, he recommended to the Royal Council that Prince Rahman be appointed his successor. After much debate, the Royal Council and the Ulema have assented to Asad's choice. Praise to Allah . . . Saudi Arabia is ruled by a new king."

The camera panned to the rear of Sheik Mansur where a group of Saudi men began chanting "Allah Akbar" with moderate enthusiasm. After the chant was repeated precisely fifteen times, Rahman and Hamud appeared at the microphone hand-in-hand. Rahman, with exaggerated dignity, spoke first.

"In the Name of Allah, the Passionate, the . . ."

Redfaced, Rahman began again. "In the Name of Allah, the Compassionate, the Merciful, we must pray for the health of my brother, Asad. We also must pray for the return of Prince Saleem. And we must seek out and punish those who have brought discredit to my brother, Saleem, and thereby return him to a place of honor."

The new king drew Hamud closer to the microphone. "The true hero of King Khalid Airport stands beside me . . . where he shall remain as long as I am king of Saudi Arabia. Prince Hamud is the choice of the Royal Council to be our new crown prince."

Though it was repeated but ten times, the chanting of "Allah Akbar" was significantly louder than before.

Releasing Hamud's hand, Rahman continued. "Of greater importance than even the announcements you have now witnessed is the decision of the Royal Council concerning the oil fields of the kingdom. To safeguard the resources of Saudi Arabia, we have asked the United States to temporarily assist the military forces of Saudi Arabia in protecting the oil fields. To ensure the long-term security of this national resource, the Royal Council also has requested our former partners in AR-AMCO to resume their previous participation in the management of the oil fields. Our American friends have reaffirmed their friendship by agreeing to this request."

In the ARAMCO compound, Fricke snickered and commented, "Nice job, Rahman."

The new king took a paper from inside his thobe. As he began to read, his voice lost its imperious edge. "It is said we are the chosen people of Allah . . . and this is true. Was not the Great Prophet born on our soil? And are we not the guardians of the centers of Islam—Mecca and Medina? For this, Allah has rewarded our kingdom with oil, and we have benefited bountifully from its sale. We have been engulfed by a sea of extravagances. It has also been said: 'One of the paradoxes of Arabian oil is that it lies thickest where it benefits the fewest.' My brothers, this imbalance *must end* . . . or our kingdom will not survive."

As Rahman paused to catch his breath, John Norlin declared, "I can't believe what I'm hearing."

"Don't," Fricke advised.

Rahman went on. "It is Allah's will that we use our immense wealth to solve the problems of our poor neighbors, many of which are Islamic. If we fail to help them, they will continue to fall under the influence of opportunists . . . and when that occurs, as we have seen in South Yemen, Afghanistan, and Ethiopia, their problems become *our* problems." The new king gazed intently into the camera to emphasize his point.

In the living room of the ARAMCO compound, Ambassador Clark softly observed, "If they only believed half of what they say."

Rahman continued. "Therefore, the Royal Council with my approval and that of Crown Prince Hamud has decided to loan our foreign reserves to the International Monetary Fund . . . with express instructions that our wealth be reloaned to the people of Third World nations. By this act of generosity, both they and we shall benefit."

"Those smart sonofabitches," muttered Fricke under his breath. He checked his watch. "Ambassador, the press conference in Washington is *already* in progress."

Clark shook his head. "It should have been scheduled before this one." He touched Dori's shoulder. "Young lady, we need your help with the radio again."

Confirming President Steiner was at his press conference, Ambassador Clark told the War Room, "This is an emergency! You've got to get this message to the President. Rahman has announced that Saudi foreign reserves will be loaned to the I.M.F. for the benefit of Third World nations. If necessary, *interrupt* President Steiner to give him my message.''

Returning to the living room, Dori and the two men saw Crown Prince Hamud speaking on the TV screen.

''. . . conflicts in the Middle East, without intervention by non-Islamic nations.''

"I think he's cute!'' exclaimed Dori. "He looks like a movie star.''

Hamud smiled. "My next words directly concern all Saudi men over the age of thirty years. The Royal Council has decreed you shall elect representatives to a Provincial Council, and this council will advise the King and me on matters concerning *all* citizens of our kingdom. With this measure, Saudi Arabia shall take its position among the democratic nations of the world.''

The Saudis in the studio, which included all of Hamud's retinue, repeated, "Allah Akbar!'' with a renewed fury.

John Norlin asked of no one in particular, "Why didn't they say anything about the massacre?''

"They did,'' Fricke told him. "In the discussion of Saleem and his national guard at the airport. It was unsaid . . . but understood.''

"It doesn't make sense to me,'' Norlin replied.

"If they're going to punish the soldiers who were at the Lockheed compound,'' explained Fricke, "it must appear they were cowards in battle.''

"They're all lying scoundrels,'' concluded Norlin.

Emory Clark shook his head at the statement. He'd been a diplomat too long to let it pass. "I don't know as if I would say that,'' reflected Clark.

"Actually, they're little different from our Italian, French, or—for that matter—Japanese *allies*. If anything, they're more clever."

No one disputed his words.

The White House

The messenger from the War Room handed the note to Jim Hoolihan, who stood behind President Steiner with the secretary of state. Skimming the message, the presidential assistant placed it on the speaker's rostrum and did not withdraw his hand until the President stopped speaking to read it. Displaying no change of expression, President Steiner resumed his press statement.

"It is my belief this will provide an enduring stability to the Persian Gulf region, much as we've seen prevail in Western Europe due to the continued presence of our military units. American Air Force and Army units have been garrisoned in Western Germany since the end of World War II, and it has been a small price to pay for nearly a half-century of prolonged peace in Europe." The unsmiling President looked up from his rostrum. "This concludes my prepared statement."

A third of the reporters in the packed auditorium broke for the doors. Those remaining, crowded closer to the podium. Allan Steiner pointed among the waving hands to a familiar face.

"Mr. President, Fred Swegles of *The Dallas Times*. Your statement was somewhat unclear concerning the responsibility for the massacre of Westerners in Riyadh. Could you elaborate?''

The President inhaled deeply. ''We're attempting to obtain additional information concerning that subject. So far, we only know what the Saudis have told us . . . that it was a senseless act by a maverick group of private Bedouin soldiers.''

Before another member of the press could be selected, the same correspondent spoke again. ''Mr. President, a source at the Saudi Arabian embassy suggested the massacre could have been related to bombs dropped by an American plane on units of the Saudi army at the capital's airport. Is this true?''

Studying his questioner a moment, President Steiner replied, ''Why didn't you ask that question in the first place, Mr. Swegles?''

Allan Steiner addressed everyone in the press room. ''In fact, we did have one aircraft drop a few bombs in an open area of Riyadh's airport for the purpose of staging a mock attack. This was necessary to confirm our military commitment to any advance agents of the invading force from South Yemen. The bombs damaged nothing other than the surface of a runway, and the Saudi military were fully aware of our mission beforehand. In addition, the Marine pilot of our aircraft reported no military units on the airfield at the time he placed the bombs, so there can be no causal relationship between the two events mentioned by Mr. Swegles. One of them never occurred.''

President Steiner returned his attention to the Texan. ''That's not the answer you were looking for, is it, Mr. Swegles?'' The reporter didn't respond.

"Let's try it from another angle," grimaced the President. "If my decision to deter the flight from Afghanistan had *not* been made, it's unlikely that those Americans would have died. Therefore, I could—conceivably—be blamed for their deaths. Whether the results of the last two days will be worth the high price we've paid is a question I shall silently debate every day for as long as I live."

After a short delay, President Steiner pointed to another hand.

"Mr. President, Bob Morrison of *The New York Times*. Why did a Saudi gunboat attack the Puller in the Persian Gulf?"

"Mr. Morrison, when we were invited to occupy Dhahran Air Base, we received assurances our forces would not be opposed by the Saudi military. In all likelihood, the attack on the Puller was due to a failure in communication. This assumes, of course, that the gunboat was manned by Saudis. Before destroying it, we didn't stop to confirm the nationality of those aboard."

The President chose another reporter.

"Mr. President, Mary Shiffren of the *Los Angeles Times*. Will the freeze of Saudi foreign reserves be lifted eventually, as was the 1979 freeze on Iranian assets?"

"I'm glad you asked that question, Ms. Shiffren. We have already informed the new leaders of Saudi Arabia that, after adequate restitution is made to the families of American victims, we'd like to see the balance of these assets go to the International Monetary Fund. Lifting the freeze depends on how the Saudis respond."

"Mr. President, Jim Christensen of the *Philadel-*

phia Inquirer. Does the freeze on Saudi assets include investments such as Suliman Olayan's minority ownership in the Chase Manhattan Bank?''

"This will depend on the needs of Third World nations," the President replied, selecting another reporter in front.

"Mr. President, Irwin Zucker of the *Miami Herald*. Did our military assist the Saudis in driving the Iranians from Kuwait?''

"We did offer protection of their oil fields when they transferred army units north," the President answered rapidly and just as quickly pointed to another correspondent.

"Mr. President, Ted Miller of the *Atlanta Constitution*. Many military experts were amazed by the lightning speed in which the unseasoned Saudi army routed the vastly more-experienced Iranian army. Can you explain how this happened, and what role other representatives of the United States might have played?''

No, I can't tell you, thought Allan Steiner, *and you know it.* He hesitated too long, signaling his search for a valid subterfuge and thereby revealing more by his delay than he would in subsequent words.

"Of course, we offered the Saudis encouragement and other minor forms of assistance. To say what was the pivotal influence would be speculative at this time.''

Miller's tone was friendly and inquisitive. "Mr. President, did you just answer my question?''

After scattered laughter, the auditorium fell silent as the press corps waited to see if more would be revealed.

"All too soon," lectured the former professor,

"you will get the details of that operation, from many divergent sources—all of whom will represent themselves as being unquestionably reliable. I'm not unfamiliar with the making of history, including the role which the press can play, and I would advise you to carefully sift your findings. Frequently, there is no infallibly identifiable cause for a historical event. It just happened."

Another hand shot up. "Mr. President, Greg Hill of the *Des Moines Register*. "Do you expect Congress to endorse our military presence in Saudi Arabia?"

The President made a tired smile. "Over the next sixty days, I'm sure we'll have a lively debate in the halls of Congress on the subject. I also believe my actions are a valid extension of the Eisenhower Doctrine—that the United States is committed to provide military assistance to any Middle Eastern country requesting such aid against overt aggression from any nation controlled by international communism." Pausing for the reporters to write down his last remark, the President then asked, "How many of you recall President Eisenhower's statement in 1957 when he declared, "The existing vacuum in the Middle East must be filled by the United States before it is filled by the Russians?" A few heads nodded.

"While I am President of the United States, the vacuum in Saudi Arabia *will not* reappear."

Applause for his words—an unusual response among the press—gradually filled the entire room. Briefly acknowledging the ovation, President Steiner gathered his notes and exited the auditorium.

After entering the Oval Office with his secretary

of state, the President stood looking out the tall windows behind his desk. Turning wearily, he caught the eye of Clayton Walters. Each man contemplated the other.

For something to say, President Steiner asked, "Who do you think will replace Derevenko?"

Walters shrugged. "Rolle only knows he's out. We don't have any idea who his successor will be yet."

Considering for a moment the disastrous consequences of the Soviet leader's decisions, the President shook his head at the thought of his own decisions. Derevenko was gone. Asad was gone. How many people were dead? He was beginning to feel the awesome and dreadful power of his office.

"Clayton . . . you know why Jimmy Carter didn't get reelected?"

His secretary of state knew to wait for the answer.

The President sneered. "The American people don't want a decent, God-fearing, honest man in this office." He paused to sit at his desk and calmly surveyed its broad expanse before continuing.

"They want an arrogant, fearless leader . . . hard-nosed in negotiations . . . unscrupulous when necessary . . ." his voice trailed off, and he thought, *everything I don't want to be.*

Walters nodded sagely. "With the exceptions of Ford and Carter, our Presidents since 1960 have been bona fide rascals . . . everyone of them. That's what this office demands."

And I'm supposed to be a professor of history, reflected Allan Steiner.

ARAMCO

"Prince Hamud, you cannot do that."

The Saudi prince smiled apologetically. "It is not I, Ambassador Clark, who determines it."

"In the eyes of the Western world," Clark tersely stated, "such an act will set your country back a hundred years!"

The smile on Hamud's face altered to one of self-amusement. He had expected the American to say a *thousand*. "It is out of my hands," Hamud replied.

"Then you must speak to those who do control it," Clark admonished.

"These are judicial matters, to be governed by the Ulema," Hamud patiently explained. "No one can tell them how to conduct such affairs."

"Hamud," interjected Irene, "why can't you go directly to the Grand Imam, as you did to gain entrance to Riyadh TV?"

"That was not a legal matter," Hamud told her.

Clark shook his head vigorously. "There *must* be another way."

"You are wrong, Ambassador. For my people, there can be no other way. All the citizens of Saudi Arabia must experience it . . . or the act will have no meaning."

"That's preposterous!" The American's words were uttered more in frustration than anger.

Hamud's voice remained calm. "Ambassador Clark, you have been in my country more than three years, yet you still do not know my people."

"Prince Hamud, it is not the end result which we dispute. It's *the uncivilized manner* of reaching that result!"

"There are many—maybe even a majority—in Saudi Arabia who think as I do . . . and we agree with Westerners that it is barbaric." Hamud frowned with his admission. "But we are controlled too often by a minority that is more vocal . . . more violent . . . more prone to follow their emotions than that which is logical."

"Why is that so?" Clark asked mildly.

"I do not know," offered Hamud. He bowed his head to avoid the American's stare and debated whether to reveal his thoughts. "Perhaps," began the Saudi, "it is due to the ancient custom which encourages the Arab to intermarry with cousins. As many as one-third of marriages in traditional Arab societies are between first cousins."

Irene stiffened in her chair. "That's unbelievable."

"Yes," nodded Hamud without looking up. "They account for an unbelievable number of hereditary diseases. Saleem comes from such a union. Two of his full-brothers are so highstrung they've been under care since childhood."

Clark spoke solemnly. "You must work to change such practices."

"We are." Hamud looked up eagerly. "Only a

generation ago, more than half the marriages in my country were between first cousins.''

The ambassador dropped his jaw in awe.

Hamud looked to Irene for her response and found downcast eyes. Standing to conclude the interview, the Saudi prince spoke with studied patience.

''Ambassador Clark, one of my reasons for coming here is to escort you back to Riyadh. I will take you before the king, and you may protest to him if you wish.''

''After what happened to the embassy,'' Clark said, ''I'm not sure I should return so soon.''

Hamud gave a small shrug. ''It was only the first floor which was damaged. You shall be my personal guest and under my protection.''

''I'll let you know tomorrow if I can return to Riyadh.'' Clark contemplated the Saudi prince a moment. ''I understand you're going over to Bahrain this evening.''

''Yes,'' smiled Hamud, ''the rulers of the Persian Gulf states are honoring your daughter and me with a lavish banquet. You may accompany us if you wish.''

Clark shook his head. ''No, I have too much work to do here. I shall see you tomorrow.''

It was one o'olock in the morning as Irene lingered with Hamud in the candlelit palace gardens of Bahrain's king. After they'd sat silently for some time on a bench before a pool of giant goldfish, Hamud reached within his thobe. When his hand came out, it held an object wrapped in black silk. He held it before her.

"This is for you."

Irene placed her palms together to receive the gift and was surprised at its heaviness.

Hamud took a corner of the black silk and gently lifted it, revealing a wide-band platinum bracelet. Inlaid around the band were 33 pear-shaped, one-carat diamonds in alternating clear and green colors. The glittering sight took away Irene's breath.

"It is fit for a queen," he whispered into her ear.

She could only voice one thought. "How much did this cost?"

He laughed at her frankness and said, "One hundred thousand of your dollars." It had cost considerably more.

Irene shook her head in disbelief.

"I want you to stay with me," Hamud told her.

"How can that be?" She looked directly at her lover. "A crown prince must take a Saudi woman as his wife."

"I need not marry," he quickly responded, taking her hands. "Do you love me?"

She made a grim smile and nodded. "You know the answer."

"Then it's settled!" Hamud ardently exclaimed.

Irene remained expressionless.

He raised an eyebrow and asked, "What is wrong?"

"Hamud, I'm not anxious to get married and have children like most women. So it isn't the fact we can't marry which bothers me"

"What bothers you then?"

She concentrated on the goldfish. "In your country, I would be as one of them."

"Them?" Hamud looked at her quizzically.

"I could not live in a society where I would be so restricted . . . even to what I wear. No movies, no theatre, no restaurants, no sports we could openly share together."

"We are trying to change much of that," he insisted. "It will be much better in the future."

Irene looked up with forlorn eyes. "I will be an old woman before that time. Saudi Arabia would be a prison to me."

"Okay," Hamud soothed, "you shall not live in Saudi Arabia. You can live in Europe . . . on the Riviera. We'll have a villa in Cannes."

"And what will you do when you're not in Cannes?"

"What do you mean?"

"Who will share your bed in Riyadh?"

"I love only you," he insisted playfully.

"I want to believe you," Irene reflected. She paused to yawn. "But I've never heard of a Saudi man who had only one woman when he could afford more . . . especially in your family."

Hamud made a short, derisive laugh. "I do not follow all the customs of my country."

"I remember reading only a few months ago," Irene said, "the words of a religious authority in Medina. He actually favored polygamy over monogamy."

Hamud's wan smile gradually disappeared.

Irene stood and wrinkled her eyes at him. "Because of what we've experienced, we have a stronger bond than just love."

Hesitantly, Hamud cupped her knees with his hands. The hands moved up the sides of her slim body, stopping at her high ribs. "This is true, my fire goddess," he murmured.

Irene gently pulled his head to her breasts . . . then turned his face to hers and kissed him lightly.

"I shall leave in the morning." She offered the bracelet back to Hamud.

Irene would never forget the shadow of sadness which for a long moment darkened his face.

He nodded to the diamond-encrusted bracelet. "It is yours," Hamud quietly told her, "for the green dress."

When her face brightened, his rakish smile came round again, and he suggested an even greater exchange.

"And let this be a night we shall always remember."

The Friday Following—11:00 A.M.

Riyadh

A liveried servant held the door of the gray limousine for the Crown Prince and Ambassador Clark. When the two men were seated, Hamud spoke the only words of their journey to his driver.

"The big square."

The *friends of Hamud*, as they were now known, also entered limousines at the foot of the broad marble steps leading from Hamud's palace. Two dozen jeeps of the Royal Guard brought up the rear.

By the time this procession was within a mile of the largest square in Riyadh, their progress was slowed by the throngs of Saudi men also moving toward the Dira. After a minute of watching the people afoot moving more quickly than his vehicle, Hamud snapped, "Stop the car! We must walk."

The Royal Guard hastily abandoned their jeeps to form a vanguard and began repeating, "Make way for the Crown Prince!" The white-uniformed soldiers reinforced their exhortations by brusquely shoving those who were slow to move aside.

When Hamud was a block from the Dira, he directed his group down a side street toward the rear of the Palace of Justice. Once inside the building which was normally closed to foreigners, Emory

Clark noted the contrast between the white-thobed crowd within and the green-tiled ceilings, walls, and floor of the massive lobby. Most of the Saudis milling about wore gold-trimmed thobes of the royal family, and with the entrance of Hamud, a momentary hush fell over them. While older members of the Saud family glared at the new Crown Prince, most of the men looked aside in respect as Hamud spearheaded a path through the lobby for his retinue. They hurried up a staircase and entered the inner sanctum of the minister of justice. Hamud presented the American ambassador to Sheik Mansur, but there was no conversation. Clark had been warned earlier the sheik neither spoke nor understood English. The three men and Hamud's friends stepped out onto a second-floor balcony overlooking the square.

The Dira was packed shoulder-to-shoulder with Saudi men in white thobes. Mingling with the buzz of their voices were blaring loudspeakers from which a muezzin recited the Koran in a steady monotone. Obliquely to his left at a distance of seventy-five yards, Clark recognized the Great Friday Mosque—the largest in Riyadh—where religious services were still in session. Two hundred and fifty yards directly across the square was the relatively modest three-story palace from which the Saudi king would observe the noon proceedings. The other fortress-like buildings fringing the quadrangle held various government ministries.

The attention of the American ambassador was drawn to the center of the northern half of the square where a fifty-by-fifty-foot wooden platform had been constructed under a watch tower—the site

where public floggings and other punishments were
meted out at noon on the Muslim holy day of the
week. Standing seven feet above the ground, the
platform was barren except for the placement of
thirty-six white towels . . . laid out in symmetrical
rows of six each. The surface of the platform appeared slightly lower on the side nearest the Great
Mosque, as if it had been built too hastily. Parked
along this side of the platform was a line of black
ambulances—their rear doors backed up to the
wooden structure. Clark turned to speak with Hamud, but the Crown Prince had moved away to
converse with others.

It was near noon in eastern Saudi Arabia. The
streets of ARAMCO were empty—its residents
driven inside by the oppressive heat. Many of them
had crowded into the meeting room of the compound's recreation center. The fortunate sat in
closely arranged rows of chairs, while others stood
at the sides and back of the large room. The weekly
nondenominational services had been relocated due
to an anticipated increase in attendance on this Friday.

The leader of the services, dressed in her custom-
ary white dress brightly embroidered with flowers,
sat in the middle of a double row of chairs facing
the gathered people. Someone from behind tapped
her shoulder, and Diana Lindsay turned her head.

Hadn't we better get started?'' suggested the
choir member. ''It's getting muggy in here.''

Checking her watch, Diana whispered back,
''Another three minutes.''

Her gaze wandered from the five vacant chairs

directly in front of her to the statuesque brunette
sitting to the immediate right of the reserved chairs.
Diana didn't recall seeing the young woman before, and she wondered how many others in the
room had come simply to catch a glimpse of their
specially invited guest.

When Diana checked her watch again, she was
surprised that ten more minutes had elapsed. As
she surveyed the waiting people, she noticed a few
parents trying to calm their restless children. Closing her eyes a moment to compose herself, Diana
stood and stepped to the head of the center aisle.

She raised her Bible and spoke in a clear, serene
voice. "We will begin today where we were interrupted one week ago—*Matthew, Chapter 5, Verse 10.*"
After pausing for others with Bibles to find the passage, Diana began to read.

"Blessed are those who hunger and thirst for
righteousness, for they shall be satisfied. Blessed
are the merciful, for they shall obtain mercy.
Blessed are the pure in heart, for they shall see
God. Blessed are the peacemakers, for they shall
be called the sons of God."

Noting a small commotion at the far end of the
aisle, Diana glanced up.

Her eyes were instantly drawn to a brilliant hue
of blue—the uniform of a man standing between a
boy and girl. Colonel Hemingway, in borrowed
Marine Corps dress blues, stood motionless and
erect with his hands braced on the shoulders of Dori
and Kevin. The twins' parents waited behind.

Diana Lindsay smiled. "I think," she genially announced, "we're being invaded again."

The others in the room quickly shifted their attention to the Marine's resplendent blue uniform. The radiance of his regalia nearly distracted them from the white bandages covering the left half of his head and his right hand.

"This time," Diana beckoned the new arrivals forward, "please join us."

Pacing slowly with shortened steps, Hemingway started down the aisle, half-supporting himself on Dori and Kevin. A couple in the back of the room began to lightly clap their hands. They continued their rhythmic applause until, with restraint, a few others joined in.

When the Marine recognized a man sitting on the aisle who had helped pull him from the burning Harrier, he paused. The civilian wore bandages over both arms. Lifting his uninjured hand off Dori's shoulder, Hemingway extended it to the man before realizing the civilian's hands were too heavily wrapped in burn dressings to be touched. The man stood as applause built in the room . . . and for the first time in his life, the Marine pilot embraced another man. After grasping the shoulder of his rescuer, Hemingway instinctively pulled the man to him in an awkward hug.

As they parted, their eyes met, and Hemingway attempted to speak his gratitude. His throat tightened instead. He offered an embarrassed smile and experienced another first.

Other faces had crowded around . . . and they too fought back tears with broad grins. *Hey,* Hemingway told himself, *cut that out.* Hands appeared to move in slow motion around him, making repeated soft impressions on his arms and shoulders. He tried to turn his misting eyes from the blurred faces, but could not. They were everywhere.

Moving down the aisle, Hemingway spotted another of his rescuers attempting to applaud with bandaged hands. The pilot stopped the twins again and gradually made his way between rows to the second rescuer.

The two men reached out to another, gripping forearm to forearm. Any words they might have spoken would have been lost in outburst of acclaim now filling the room.

Returning to the aisle, Hemingway raised his chin, no longer trying to fight his natural emotions. A salty tear stung the still raw flesh of his left cheek. He and the twins made their way to the front of the room as the ovation began to abate. Arriving at the reserved chairs, Hemingway shuffled his escorts to gain the seat beside Sandi. He avoided her eyes, trying to gain control of his own.

The release of sentiment in the room provided a peculiar cleansing effect for those present, followed by an uneasy silence—a short moment forever etched in their memories.

Diana Lindsay said with a struggle, "Let us pray silently."

In the absolute stillness which followed, Hemingway reached into a pocket of his uniform and withdrew a small box. When it was open, he turned to Sandi. Her head was bowed with closed eyes. Melted mascara streaked her cheeks.

He leaned nearer and whispered. "I pray . . . you'll marry me."

Blinking her eyes, Sandi slowly looked up and followed his gaze down to the ring. She remained thoughtful a few seconds, tried a skittish grin, and whispered back, "Is it Marine Corps issue?"

He nodded seriously. It was. Or nearly so, as a friend had purchased it from the exchange on the Constellation.

When Diana Lindsay raised her bowed head, she saw the brunette lightly brush the Marine's lips with her own.

In a voice that faltered at first, the woman in the flowered white dress resumed the *Sermon on the Mount:*

"You have heard it said, 'You shall love your neighbor and hate your enemy.' But I say to you, love your enemies and pray for those who persecute you, so that you may be sons of your Father who is in Heaven. For if you love only those who love you, what reward have you?"

"Judge not, that you be not judged. For with the judgment you pronounce, you will be judged. And the measure you give will be the measure you get."

"Ask, and it will be given you. Seek, and you will find. Knock, and it will be opened to you. For every one who asks receives, and he who seeks finds, and to him who knocks, it will be opened."

"And in praying, do not heap up empty phrases, thinking they will be heard for their many words. Your Father knows what you need before you ask Him. Pray then like this . . ."

The voices in the room joined in a resounding recitation of *The Lord's Prayer*.

Hamud returned to the side of Emory Clark and
glanced at his watch. "It will be soon," he announced. "Watch the doors of the Great Mosque."

After concentrating on the multiple fifteen-foot
high doors of the mosque for some time, Clark's
attention wandered over the motionless mass of
people before him. He guessed the Dira now held
between fifteen thousand and twenty thousand men.
A murmur rose above the din of the crowd, drawing his attention back to the mosque. The doors
had opened, and the harangue of the loudspeakers
abruptly halted. Clark watched as several thousand
more men exited the mosque and added to the crush
of the crowd.

Directly under his balcony, Clark heard harsh
voices shouting orders and two columns of soldiers
carrying Uzi submachine guns formed a path from
the Palace of Justice to the raised platform. When
they reached it, a Saudi army officer climbed its
steps and paced across the platform several times
before facing the Palace of Justice and saluting.

Through the pathway between the double column of soldiers, additional armed soldiers passed
and took up a perimeter around the sides of the
wooden platform. Clark heard more orders barked
from below and saw the first of a line of six prisoners wearing sparkling white thobes hobble from
the Palace of Justice. The first man was flanked by
two guards, neither of whom touched their charge.

Clark noted the first captive was missing his right
hand and was surprised no bandage covered the

stump. His arms were tightly bound to his sides by rope at elbow height. The man shuffled forward slowly in leg irons, as if in a daze.

The American quickly examined the forearms of the other prisoners as they came in sight. Each man was also missing the right hand, and one lacked his left hand as well. Reaching into his jacket, Clark pulled out his glasses and leaned over the balcony to see better. None of the men wore dressings over their mutilations. Having heard the account of Hamud's exposure of the guilty national guardsmen at the Riyadh television building, he also knew the mandatory punishment for Arabs caught stealing was the removal of a hand. Clark was perplexed now, as the wrist-stumps failed to display any redness from their amputation wounds.

Noticing Clark's close scrutiny of the six captives, Hamud leaned closer. "What is it, Mr. Ambassador?"

Clark considered whether to ask his own question. After a lengthy pause, he commented, "They appear to be drugged."

"Yes," nodded Hamud benevolently. "As a kindness, we give them something to calm their nerves."

When the first of the shuffling prisoners reached the platform, Clark saw why each of them had a two-guard escort. The square stilled as the soldiers gripped the arms of the first shackled captive and half-lifted him up the steps.

The six prisoners were led to the line of white towels alongside the lower edge of the platform. Each of them faced the Great Mosque and voluntarily fell to a kneeling position on a towel.

A soldier then stood over each kneeling man and removed the prisoner's gutra, setting it beside the towel. Using both hands to grip the collars of their charges, the soldiers jerked at the cotton shifts until they'd torn the material halfway down the back of each captive. With this act, the massed throng surged forward and began repeating, "ALLAH AKBAR! ALLAH AKBAR!"

The kneeling men lowered themselves even more, coming as near to the position of Muslim prayer as their bound arms would permit. To Clark's amazement, the escorting soldiers stepped back from their prisoners and marched off the platform. The American did not realize the hypnotic effect of the crowd's chanting on the prostrate men. The six captives *of the crowd* tucked their chins to their chests and would not move again.

The next six men to leave the Palace of Justice were tall, broad-shouldered Saudis who also wore the traditional white thobe . . . with three accouterments. Across their left shoulders was a wide black sash, and strapped to each waist was a large caliber pistol. Swinging from their left hips were the long crescent-shaped scabbards of their profession.

The tempo of the crowd's chanting increased slightly as the black-sashed men mounted the platform and unsheathed their great curved blades as they strode toward the kneeling men. The finely polished swords glistened in the sun as the tall Saudis took up positions to the right of each prisoner. After spreading their legs for balance, the tall men slowly lowered the long blades to a position about eight inches above the necks of their respective victims.

Emory Clark considered whether to step off the balcony rather than witness more of the spectacle. Deciding instead to close his eyes at the last moment, he glanced toward Hamud.

The Crown Prince visibly shook as he imitated the other Saudis on the balcony. As if in a trance, Hamud feverishly repeated the Arab words for, ''God is great! God is great!''

Returning his eyes to the wooden platform, it was too late for Clark to avert them.

Flashes of steel slashed downward. He clearly heard the sickening thump of metal on flesh. Four heads rolled away. The other two dangled at grotesque angles. Clark clamped his eyes shut as thick spumes of crimson fluid spurted from the stumps. The solid arcs of red blood hung in the air for a brief moment before the six bodies collapsed in lifeless heaps.

The roar of the satisfied crowd died . . . to be replaced by vigorous applause. The American reopened his eyes and watched as the executioners knelt beside their victims and spat upon their dripping blades before wiping them clean on the sleeves of the executed.

When the executioners withdrew, a doctor came up the steps to complete the medieval drama. He was followed by the guard escorts of the six captives. Each pair of guards carried a crude wooden stretcher. The doctor went through the motions of examining the bodies with a stethoscope.

After wrapping the heads of the captives in their gutras, the soldiers dumped the remains onto the wooden stretchers and handed them down to the waiting ambulance attendants. The white towels upon which the six men had knelt were used to hastily mop up the blood that had not already poured off the platform.

When the stage was again bare of men, Emory Clark stared, transfixed at the blood dripping off its edge. Six more prisoners emerged from the Palace of Justice and began to shuffle to their fate. After examining the healed wrist-stumps of their amputated hands, the American ambassador finally asked his question of Hamud.

"Were those prisoners members of your National Guard?"

The Crown Prince stiffened. He did not reply . . . or even turn his head.

It didn't matter.

The dogmas of the quiet past are inadequate to the stormy present. The occasion is piled high with difficulty. And we must rise with the occasion. As our case is new, so we must think anew, and act anew. We must disenthrall ourselves.

Abraham Lincoln, 1861

Afterword

Together with the late General Keith McCutcheon (the first four-star general in U.S. Marine aviation), I was one of the principal American generals during the period of 1970–1972 to push through the procurement of the AV-8A Harrier—one of the most remarkable weapons in the arsenal of the United States.

This is the first novel, of which I am aware, that reveals the great versatility of this marvelous piece of technology. As the reader learns, the AV-8B (the most recent version) can outmaneuver any fighter in the world within its altitude. This is due to its superior turning capability, coupled with the dexterity to attain a near-instant hover in midair.

Detractors of this aircraft said the Harrier would operate under too many restrictions, such as limited airspeed, range, altitude, and payload. They were proved wrong in the air war over the Falklands, when only a V-STOL aircraft proved capable of landing on the primitive land conditions offered by those remote islands. More important, the British Harriers demonstrated they could operate off a small assault carrier at sea in the worst weather—under conditions which would normally ground all other naval aircraft. It is a fact that the

Harrier can operate from any ship, including an *oil tanker*, which offers a small landing platform.

We are all aware of the volatile situation in the Persian Gulf today. While GOOD FRIDAY is an entertaining novel, I believe one of its important messages is how we and our Arab allies can defuse some of the explosiveness in this strategic, oil-rich region.

Major General Homer S. Hill, USMC (Ret.)
Deputy Chief of Staff, Marine Corps Aviation
and
Vice Chief of Naval Operations (Op-05M)
1970–1972

Acknowledgments

Too much of this novel is already true:

- the oilfields of Russia have produced decreasing amounts of oil since the early 1980s.
- Russian military forces are stationed in South Yemen, 500 miles south of the major oilfields of Saudi Arabia.
- within the Persian Gulf (adjacent to the Saudi oilfields), the U.S. Navy has maintained a small assault carrier whose complement consists of 1800 Marines, 36 Sea Stallion helicopters, and 9 Harrier attack jets, plus a few accompanying small ships.
- mistrustful of its own security forces, the royal family in Saudi Arabia has hired three brigades of Pakistanis to guard their palaces.
- Cuban soldiers were flown into South Yemen in 1979 from Ethiopia to suppress South Yemen soldiers who remained loyal to their assassinated president.
- East Germans have managed concentration camps in South Yemen in recent years.
- in December 1979, three Soviet airborne divisions stormed into Afghanistan, murdering the Marxist leader then in power and installing Babrak Karmal, who promptly issued a call to

Moscow for Soviet troops who were already in his country.

* since the first Marxist government took office in Kabul (1978), more than 27,000 Afghani have been executed in a concentration camp (Poli Charki) outside Kabul.

* among the 18 Arab nations, only South Yemen has a lower literacy rate (12 percent) than that of Saudi Arabia (15 percent).

* in 1986, authorities in Jordan reported that 33 percent of all marriages were to first cousins. Sari Nasser (head of the sociology department at the University of Jordan) believes that such statistics represent a decline from a few years ago, when he estimates that 80 percent of all marriages involved cousins.

While serving as the Saudi minister of petroleum, Sheik Ahmed Yamani cautioned, "The Soviets may someday, when they become net oil importers, think our oil is in their strategic interests." Most Americans probably share my general feelings that we should not *overly* involve ourselves with the affairs of other nations; however, at times this generalization may prove a bit shortsighted.

In his book, *ARABIA, The Gulf and the West,* John B. Kelly aptly states, ". . . the temptation for the Russians to acquire by political or military means what they cannot afford to purchase must be a strong one. It can only be made stronger by the consideration that the acquisition of preferential access to the Gulf's oil would enable the Soviet Union to dictate the terms upon which oil would thereafter be supplied to the West."

I extend my gratitude to the men and women who permitted me to interview them concerning their experiences working and living in Saudi Arabia. Prudence dictates that their names not be listed herein. I would also like to express my appreciation to the men in uniform who gave generously of their time during the writing of the military action described in the book. And thank you, Gigi, for your able assistance in the editing and juxtaposition of events in this embroiled story.

RLH

List of Main Characters

King ASAD—Saudi monarch

Captain CARTER—air wing commander, *Constellation*

Emory CLARK—American ambassador to Riyadh

Premier DEREVENKO—Soviet premier

Senator FARRELL—U.S. Senate majority leader

Louis FRICKE—military attaché, Riyadh embassy

Colonel HABIB—Saudi national guard officer

Prince HAMUD—Saudi prince

Lt. Colonel HEMINGWAY—Marine air group commander

Lisa HILL—ham radio operator

General HUERING—Commandant, U.S. Marine Corps

Jim HOOLIHAN—special assistant to the President

IRENE—American woman from French Riviera

Sheik MANSUR—Grand Imam of Riyadh

General MORRISON—Chief of staff, U.S. Air Force

Dori NORLIN—American girl in ARAMCO compound

Kevin NORLIN—Dori's twin brother

Prince RAHMAN—Saudi defense minister

Edward ROLLE—CIA director

Colonel ROMANOV—Russian commander, South Yemen fight

Prince SALEEM—Crown Prince of Saudi Arabia

Edward SNELL—Speaker of the House

General STEEL—Chairman, Joint Chiefs of Staff

Allan STEINER—the President of the United States

Colonel TUPOLOV—Russian commander, Afghanistan flight

Clayton WALTERS—Secretary of State

Senator WINSLOW—Senate minority leader

About the Author

Robert Lawrence Holt is the author of seven books, two of which were Book-of-the-Month Club selections. His first novel, *Sweetwater: Gunslinger 201* was a winner of the Book of the Year award from the Aviation/Space Writers Association.